Shelter from
the

RAEANNE THAYNE

MILLS & BOON®

Pure reading pleasure™

First published in Great Britain 2008
Large Print edition 2008
Harlequin Mills & Boon Limited,
Eton House, 18-24 Paradise Road,
Richmond, Surrey TW9 1SR

© RaeAnne Thayne 2007

ISBN: 978 0 263 20152 9

Set in Times Roman 17 on 20 pt.
34-1208-61350

Printed and bound in Great Britain
by CPI Antony Rowe, Chippenham, Wiltshire

RAEANNE THAYNE

finds inspiration in the beautiful northern Utah mountains, where she lives with her husband and children. Her books have won numerous honours, including a RITA® Award nomination from Romance Writers of America and a Career Achievement award from *Romantic Times BOOKreviews* magazine. RaeAnne loves to hear from readers and can be reached through her website at www.raeannethayne.com or at PO Box 6682 North Logan, UT 84341, USA.

To Darcy Rhodes,
for sharing your singing and
your smiles, for changing diapers
and telling jokes and helping us
take unforgettable journeys we
once thought were impossible.
You'll always be part of our family!

Chapter 1

"Would you take your shirt off, please?"

Under other circumstances—and from just about any other woman—Daniel Galvez might have been tempted to take those words as a rather enticing request.

From Dr. Lauren Maxwell, he knew all too well she meant nothing suggestive—as much as he might wish otherwise.

He sighed, detesting this whole ordeal, even as he knew he had no choice but to comply. His right hand went to the buttons of his uniform and he wrestled them free, uncomfortably aware of her watching him out of those intense blue eyes that seemed to miss nothing.

He had to work hard to hide a wince as he shrugged out of his shirt, mentally bracing himself for the moment she would touch him with those cool fingers.

The pain didn't worry him. He had coped with much worse than a little scratch on the arm. Handling Lauren and the feelings she always stirred up in him was another matter entirely.

She watched him take off his shirt, her eyes veiled as they always seemed to be in his presence, and he wondered what she saw. The dirt-poor Mexican kid on the school bus in the fraying, too-small jeans and the threadbare coat? Or the harsh, hard-as-nails cop she must hate?

Those cool, lovely features didn't reveal even a hint of whatever she might think of him. Just as well, he thought. He had a feeling he was better off not knowing.

"Sorry to come in so late," he said as he pulled his blood-soaked shirt away. "I wouldn't have stopped if I hadn't seen the lights on as I was driving past."

She raised an eyebrow, though her attention remained fixed on his reason for being in her examination room of the Moose Springs Medical Clinic. "That's quite a nasty laceration you've got there, Sheriff. What were you going to do about it, if you weren't going to stop here? Stitch it up yourself?"

If he were capable of such a feat, he probably would have tried rather than finding himself in this uncomfortable position. "I figured I would catch a minute to run into the emergency clinic in Park City later."

That was still his preferred option. But since he was missing two deputies this weekend in a department that was already understaffed, he didn't have that luxury.

This was his third night of double shifts and he just couldn't spare the personal leave to drive the half hour to Park City, sit in the emergency clinic there while he waited his turn for a couple hours among all the banged-up skiers and tourists with altitude sickness, then drive a half hour back to Moose Springs.

With the ski season in full swing, Park City in January was crazy anyway—throw in an independent film festival that drew thousands of Hollywood types and their entourages, and he would just about rather chew tire spikes then spend time there if he didn't have to.

Even if that meant baring his chest for Lauren Maxwell.

"You know I'm always on call for you and your deputies if you need me," she said. Though her voice was low and polite, he still felt a pinch of reprimand.

She stepped forward, close enough that he could smell the subtle, intoxicating scent of jasmine and vanilla that always seemed to cling to her. She didn't touch him yet, just continued to study the jagged three-inch cut on his upper arm that was beginning to throb like hell.

"How did you say you were injured?"

"Bar fight down at Mickey's. Some joker from out of town got mad when Johnny Baldwin kept playing 'Achy Breaky Heart' on the jukebox."

"Uh-oh. He and Carol are fighting again?"

"Apparently. By about the sixth go-around, the tourist had had enough of Billy Ray and tried to physically prevent Johnny from putting in another quarter."

"I hope you didn't arrest him for that. Sounds like justifiable assault to me."

A muscle twitched in his cheek at her dry tone, though it was taking most of his concentration to keep his mind on the story and away from how incredible it felt to have Lauren Maxwell's hands on him, even in a clinical setting.

"Most of the bar probably would have backed the guy up at first. But of course he had to go and push his luck. He went just a bit too far and insulted both Johnny and any woman stupid enough to go out with him in the first place. And of course three of Carol's brothers happened to be sitting at the other end of the bar and they didn't take too kindly to that. By the time I got there, everybody in the place was having a good old time throwing punches and smashing chairs. I was trying to take the tourist into custody, mostly for his own protection, when his buddy came after me with the business end of a broken beer bottle."

"I'm sorry."

He lifted his uninjured shoulder. "Hazard of the job."

"Should I be expecting more casualties?"

"From what I could tell, the damage seemed to be mostly bloody noses and a couple of black eyes. The paramedics showed up just in case but I appeared to get the worst of it."

"I imagine Mickey's not too crazy about having his bar ripped apart."

"You know Mickey. He was right in the middle of it all."

She probed the edge of his wound and he couldn't hide a grimace.

"Sorry," she murmured, stepping away. "I'm going to have to clean it up a little before I can put in any stitches. Sit tight while I grab a suture kit and some antiseptic."

"No problem."

The moment she left the room, he huffed out the breath he hadn't realized he'd been holding. Okay, so this hadn't been one of his better ideas. He should have just accepted his fate and driven into Park City, to hell with the jam it would put in his schedule.

Being here alone in the medical clinic with Lauren after hours was far too intimate, much too dangerous for his peace of mind.

He sighed, frustrated once again at this tension that always simmered between them.

It hadn't always been this way, but the events of five years earlier had changed everything. Lauren was still cordial, unfailingly polite, but she didn't treat him with the same warmth she gave everyone else. Every interaction between them seemed awkward and tense.

Though they grew up a few blocks away from each other, they may as well have been on different planets when they were kids. For one thing, she was three years younger. At thirty and thirty-three, now that didn't seem to make much difference. But when he was thirteen and trying his best to find his place in the world, a ten-year-old girl held about as much interest to him as learning the fox-trot.

Beyond that, they had been worlds apart demographically. She had been the smart and beautiful daughter of the town mayor—his dad's boss—and he had been the son of Mexican immigrants who never had enough of anything to go around but love.

He had tried to cross that social divide only once, the year he finished out his football scholarship and graduated from college. He had come home to work construction at her father's company for the summer before starting his police-officer training in the fall and he suddenly couldn't help noticing smart, pretty little Lauren Maxwell had grown into a beautiful college freshman, home for the summer between terms.

One night she had stopped by her father's office at the same time he dropped in after a job to pick up his paycheck. They had talked a little, flirted a little—though in retrospect, that had been one-sided on his part—and he had ended up asking her to dinner.

She had refused him firmly and decisively, almost horror-stricken, leaving him no room at all to maneuver around his abruptly deflated ego.

He could survive a little rejection. Hell, it had probably been good for him, a college jock far too full of himself.

If that had been the end of it, he imagined they could have salvaged at least a casual friendship over the years, especially after they both returned to settle in Moose Springs. She was the town's only doctor and he was the sheriff, so they were bound to interact sometimes.

But what came after had effectively destroyed any chance he had of claiming even that.

There was too much history between them, too many secrets, for anything but this awkwardness.

He wasn't sure how much she knew. Enough, obviously, for her to simmer about it. If she knew the whole truth, she would despise him even more. Somehow that knowledge did nothing to squash the attraction that always seethed under his skin, the edginess he couldn't seem to shake.

The door opened suddenly and she returned carrying a tray of bandages and suture supplies. He must have done a credible job of hiding his thoughts. She gave him a smile that almost looked genuine—until he saw the murkiness in her blue eyes.

"You'll have to sit down so I can reach your arm. You can rest it on this table."

He hesitated only a moment before he sat down where she indicated and thrust out his arm. The cut was jagged and ugly and still stung like hell, but he knew it looked worse than it really was.

Still, he winced when she pulled out a needle to numb the area. He would far rather face a dozen broken beer bottles than a needle. She caught his expression and gave him a reassuring smile. "It will only sting for a minute, I promise."

Feeling foolish and itchy at her nearness, he stoically endured the shot, then the gentle brush of her hands as she washed off the blood with Betadine and went to work stitching him up. He finally had to focus on a painting on the wall of two children on a beach eating ice cream and couldn't help wishing for a little cold refreshment to offset the heat of her fingers touching his skin.

"You're very good at that."

She didn't look up from her careful suturing. "Thanks. I considered a surgical specialty when I was in med school but I decided I wanted to see more of my patients than their insides."

"Lucky for us, I guess."

She didn't answer and the silence stretched

between them. He scrambled around for another topic of conversation and grabbed the first one that came to him. "How's your mother?"

This time her gaze did flash to his, her expression unreadable. "Good. The warm St. George climate agrees with her. She's become quite a rabid golfer now that she can play all year."

He tried to picture soft and prim Janine Maxwell ripping up the golf course and couldn't quite get a handle on it. But then he never would have pictured Lauren Maxwell choosing to practice in quiet Moose Springs, when she could have gone anywhere else in the world.

Oddly, she seemed to follow his train of thought. "Mom wants me to sell the clinic and open up another one in southern Utah."

He didn't like the sudden panic spurting through him at the thought of her leaving. "Will you?"

Her hair brushed his arm as she shook her head. "Not a chance," she said firmly. "Moose Springs is my home and I'm not going anywhere."

He didn't miss the defiance in her voice and he fully understood the reason for it. Things couldn't always be easy for her here—he knew there were some in town who would rather drive the thirty-five minutes to Park City for their medical care than walk through the doors of any clinic run by the daughter of the town's biggest crook.

The good people of Moose Springs hadn't taken R. J. Maxwell's embezzlement of more than a million dollars of their hard-earned money very kindly. Even five years after his death, there were those who still carried a pretty hefty grudge.

Most people in town didn't blame the daughter for the father's sins, but he had heard enough whispers and veiled innuendos to know *most* didn't mean *all*. A certain percentage of the population wasn't as fair-minded.

If the full story ever emerged, he knew that percentage would probably increase dramatically.

Lauren's own mother had been quick to escape Moose Springs after the scandal broke.

He couldn't understand why Lauren seemed determined to remain in town despite the ugly blotches on her family's laundry.

"That should do it," she said after a moment, affixing a bandage to the spot. "I'll write you a prescription for a painkiller and an antibiotic, just to be on the safe side."

"Just the antibiotic," he said, shrugging back into his ruined uniform shirt.

"That's a nasty laceration. You might be surprised at the residual pain tomorrow."

"I'll take an aspirin if it gets too bad."

She rolled her eyes but before she could speak, his communicator buzzed with static and a moment later he heard his dispatcher's voice.

"Chief, I've got Dale Richins on the line," Peggy Wardell said. "Says he was driving home from his sister's in Park City and blew a tire."

"He need help with it?"

"Not with the tire. But when he went in the back to get the spare, he found a girl hiding in the camper shell of his pickup."

He blinked at that unexpected bit of information. "A girl?"

"Right. She's beat up pretty good, Dale says, and tried to escape when he found her but she collapsed before she could get far. She only *hablas* the *español,* apparently. Thought I'd better let you know."

He grabbed for his blood-soaked coat, sudden dread congealing in his gut. One of the hazards of working in a small town was the fear every time a call like this came in, he didn't know who he might find at the scene.

He knew just about everyone in the growing Latino community around Moose Springs and hated the possibility that someone he knew—someone's *hija* or *hermana*—might have been attacked.

"Thanks, Peg. Tell Dale I can be there in five minutes or so."

"Right."

He headed for the door, then stopped short when he realized Lauren was right on his heels, passing a medical kit from hand to hand as she shoved the opposite hand into her parka.

"What do you think you're doing?" he asked.

"I'm coming with you," she said, that Lauren stubbornness in her voice. "Sounds like you've got a victim who will need medical care and if I go with you, I can be on scene faster than the volunteer paramedics."

He didn't want to take the time to argue with her—not when a few seconds consideration convinced him the idea was a good one. Lauren was more qualified to offer better medical care than anything the volunteer medics could provide.

"Let's go then," he said, leading the way out into the drizzling snow.

Daniel drove through the slushy roads with his lights flashing but his siren quiet, at a speed that had her hanging on to her medical kit with both hands.

She gritted her teeth as he hit one of the town's

famous potholes and her head slammed against the headrest.

"Sorry," he said, though he barely looked at her.

Nothing new there. Daniel seldom looked at her, not if he could help himself. She was glad for it, she told herself. She didn't want him looking too closely at her. He already knew too much about her, more than just about anyone else in town—she didn't want him aiming those piercing brown eyes too far into her psyche.

She gripped her bag more tightly as he drove toward the scene, trying not to notice how big and hard and dangerous he seemed under these conditions.

Sheriff Daniel Galvez was not a man any sane person would want to mess with. He was six feet three inches and two hundred and ten pounds of pure muscle. Not that she made note of his vital statistics during the rare times she had treated him or anything—it was just hard to miss a man so big who was still as tough and physically imposing as the college football player he'd been a decade earlier.

Beside him, she always felt small and fragile, a feeling she wasn't particularly crazy about. She *wasn't* small, she was a respectable five feet six inches tall and a healthy one hundred and fifteen pounds. It was only his size that dwarfed her. And she wasn't fragile, either. She had survived med school, a grueling residency and, just a few months later, crippling shock and disbelief at the chaos her father left in his wake.

She shoved away thoughts of her father as Daniel pulled the department's Tahoe to a stop behind a battered old pickup she recognized as belonging to Dale Richins. The old rancher stood behind his camper shell, all but wringing his hands.

He hurried to them the moment Daniel shut off the engine. "The little girl is inside the camper shell of my truck. I had a horse blanket in there. I guess that's what she was hiding under. Looks like you brought medical help.

Good. From what I can see, she's beat up something terrible."

He looked at Lauren with a little less suspicion than normal, but she didn't have time to be grateful as she headed for the back of the pickup. Daniel was right behind her and he didn't wait for her to ask for help—he just lifted her up and over the tailgate and into the truck bed.

He aimed the heavy beam of his flashlight inside as she made her careful way to the still form lying motionless under a grimy blanket that smelled of livestock and heaven knows what else.

She pulled out her flashlight, barely able to make out the battered features of a Latina girl.

"She's so young," Lauren exclaimed as she immediately went to work examining her. Though it was hard to be sure with all the damage, she didn't think the girl was much older than fourteen or fifteen.

"Do you know her?" Daniel asked, leaning in and taking a closer look.

"I don't think so. You?"

"She doesn't look familiar. I don't think she's from around here."

"Whoever she is, she's going to need transport to the hospital. This is beyond what I can handle at the clinic."

"How urgent?" Daniel asked from outside the pickup. "Ambulance or LifeFlight to the University of Utah?"

She considered the situation. "Her vitals are stable and nothing seems life-threatening at this point. Send for an ambulance," she decided.

She lifted the girl's thin T-shirt, trying to look for anything unusual in the dim light. She certainly found it.

"Sheriff, she's pregnant," she exclaimed.

He leaned inside, his expression clearly shocked. "Pregnant?"

"I'd guess about five or six months along."

She moved her stethoscope and was relieved to hear a steady fetal heartbeat. She started to palpate the girl's abdomen when suddenly her patient's eyes flickered open. Even in the dim light inside the camper shell, Lauren could see panic chase across those battered features. The girl cried out and flailed at Lauren as she tried to scramble up and away from her.

"Easy, sweetheart. Easy," Lauren murmured. Her skills at Spanish were limited but she tried her best. "I'm not going to hurt you. I'm here to help you and your baby."

The girl's breathing was harsh and labored, but her frantic efforts to fight Lauren off seemed to ease and she watched her warily.

"I'm Lauren. I'm a doctor," she repeated in Spanish, holding up her stethoscope. "What's your name?"

Through swollen, discolored eyes, the girl looked disoriented and suspicious, and didn't answer for several seconds.

"Rosa," she finally said, her voice raspy and strained. "Rosa Vallejo."

Lauren smiled as calmly as if they were meeting for brunch. It was a skill she'd learned early in medical school—pretend you were calm and in control and your patients will assume you are. "Hello, Rosa Vallejo. I'm sorry you're hurt but an ambulance is on the way for you, okay? We're going to get you to the hospital."

"No! No hospital. Please!"

The fear in the girl's voice seemed to hitch up a notch and she tried to sit up again. Lauren touched her arm, for comfort and reassurance as much as to hold her in place. "You've been hurt. You need help. You need to make sure your baby is all right."

"No. No. I'm fine. I must go."

She lunged to climb out of the truck bed but Daniel stood blocking the way, looking huge and imposing, his badge glinting in the dim light. The girl froze, a whimper in her throat and a look of abject terror in her eyes. *"No policía. No policía!"*

She seemed incoherent with fear, struggling hysterically to break free of Lauren's hold. Daniel finally reached in to help, which only seemed to upset the girl more.

"Hold her while I find something in my kit to calm her," Lauren ordered. "She's going to injure herself more if I don't."

A moment later, she found what she was looking for. Daniel held the girl while Lauren injected her with a sedative safe for pregnant women. A moment later, the medicine started to work its calming effect on her panicked patient and she sagged back against the horse blankets just as the wail of the ambulance sounded outside.

Lauren let out a sigh of relief and started to climb out of the truck bed. When Daniel reached to lift her out, she suddenly remembered his injury. She ignored his help and climbed out on her own.

"You're going to break open all those lovely stitches if you don't take it easy."

"I'm fine," he said firmly, just as the volunteer paramedics hurried over, medical bags slung over their shoulders.

"Hey, Mike, Pete," Lauren greeted them with a smile.

"You trying to take over our business now, Doc?" Pete asked her with a wink.

"No way. You guys are the experts at triage here. I happened to be stitching up the sheriff at the clinic after the big brawl at Mickey's bar. When he received this call, I rode along to see if I could help."

"Busy night for all of us. What have we got?"

Daniel stepped closer to hear her report and Lauren tried not to react to his overwhelming physical presence.

She gave them Rosa's vitals. "I have a young patient who appears to be approximately twenty weeks pregnant. It was tough to do a full assessment under these conditions, but she looks like she's suffering multiple contusions and lacerations, probably the result of a beating. She appears to be suffering from exposure. I have no idea how long she's been in the back of Dale's pickup. Maybe an hour, maybe more. Whether that contributed to her hysteria, I can't say, but I do know she's not very crazy about authority figures right now. Seeing the sheriff set her off, so we may have to use restraints in the ambulance on our way to Salt Lake City."

"You riding along?" Mike Halling asked.

"If I won't be in the way."

"You know we've always got room for you, Doc."

She stood back while he and Pete Zabrisky quickly transferred the girl to the stretcher then lifted it into the ambulance.

"I'm guessing she must have climbed in the back of the truck in Park City, or wherever Dale might have stopped on the way. Though I'm pretty sure the attack didn't happen here, I'm going to put one of my deputies to work processing the scene," Daniel told her while they waited in the stinging sleet for the paramedics to finish loading Rosa into the bus.

"All right," she answered.

"I won't be far behind you. I'd like to question her once she's been treated." He paused. "I can give you a ride back to town when we're done, if you need it."

She nodded and climbed in after Mike and Pete. Maybe she had a problem with authority figures, too. That must be why her stomach fluttered and her heartbeat accelerated at the prospect of more time in the company of the unnerving Daniel Galvez.

Chapter 2

Watching Dr. Lauren Maxwell in action was more fascinating to him than the Final Four, the World Series and the Super Bowl combined. As long as she wasn't working on him and he didn't have to endure having her hands on him, Daniel wouldn't mind watching her all day.

As he stepped back to let the ambulance pull past him, with its lights flashing through the drizzle of snow, he could see Lauren through the back windows as she talked to the paramedics in what he imagined was that brisk, efficient voice she used when directing patient care.

In trauma situations, Lauren always seemed completely in control. He never would have guessed back in the day that she would make such a wonderful physician.

He still found it amazing that the prim little girl on the school bus with her pink backpacks and her fake-fur-trimmed coats and her perfectly curled blond ringlets seemed to have no problem wading through blood and guts and could handle herself with such quiet but confident expertise, no matter the situation.

She loved her work. It was obvious every time Daniel had the chance to see her in action. Medicine wasn't a job with Lauren Renee Maxwell, it was more like a sacred calling.

In the five years since she'd come back to Moose Springs and opened her clinic, he had watched her carefully. Like many others, at first he had expected her to fail. She was the spoiled, pampered daughter of the man who had been the town's wealthiest citizen. How could she possibly have the stamina to cope with all the gritty realities of small-town doctoring?

Like almost everyone else, he had quickly figured out that there was more to Lauren than anybody might have guessed. Over the years, her clinic had become a strong, vital thread in the community fabric.

They were all lucky to have her—and so was that young girl in the back of the ambulance.

"What am I supposed to do now?" Dale Richins asked, his wide, grizzled features concerned.

"We're going to need a statement from you. The address of your sister's house in Park City, any place you might have stopped between there and here. That kind of thing."

"I can tell you where LouAnn lives. She's on the edge of town, the only part the old-timers can afford anymore, with all the developers trying to buy everybody out. But I can tell you right now, I didn't stop a single place after I left her house. Headed straight home. I don't know if I even would have known that girl was back there if I hadn't stopped to fix the flat. She would have likely froze to death."

"You did the right thing, trying to help her."

"What else was I supposed to do? Little thing like that." He shook his head. "Just makes me sick, someone could hurt her and leave her to find her own way in the cold. Especially if she's pregnant like the doc said. It's got to be only eight or nine degrees out here. I can't imagine how cold it was in the back of that drafty old camper shell while I was going sixty-five miles an hour on the interstate. It's a wonder that little girl didn't freeze solid before I found her."

"Yeah, it was lucky you found her when you did."

"Who do you figure might have done this to her?"

"I couldn't guess right now until I have a chance to talk to her. I imagine she was probably looking for some way to escape when she stumbled onto your truck and camper shell. The lock's broken, I see."

"That old thing's been busted since before you quit your fancy job in the city and came home. But yeah, that makes sense that she was looking for a way out."

"So either she was injured somewhere near your sister's house or she stumbled on your truck sometime after the beating. I'll know better after I can interview her."

Dale cleared his throat. "You let me know if she needs anything, won't you? I can't afford much, but I could help some with her doctor bills and whatnot."

He couldn't help being touched at the crusty old rancher's obvious concern for his stowaway. Most of the time, Dale was hard-edged and irascible, cranky to everyone. Maybe Rosa reminded him of his three granddaughters or something.

"Thanks," he answered. "That's real decent of you."

"Least I can do."

"There's Deputy Hendricks," Daniel said as another department SUV approached. "She'll take a statement from you with the particulars of your sister's address and all, and then she can drive you home when you're finished."

"What the hell for? I can drive myself home."

"I'm sorry, Dale, but we're going to have to take your truck to the garage down at the station to see if we can find any evidence in the back. It's standard procedure in cases like this."

The rancher didn't look too thrilled with that piece of information. "Don't I have any kind of choice here?"

"You want us to do everything we can to find out who hurt that girl, don't you?"

"I suppose…"

"You'll have it back by morning, I promise."

That didn't seem to ease Dale's sour look, but the rancher seemed to accept the inevitable.

"You heading to the hospital now?" he asked. At Daniel's nod, he pointed a gnarled finger at him. "You make sure R.J.'s daughter treats that girl right."

Though he knew it was a foolish reflex, Daniel couldn't help but stiffen at the renewed animosity in the rancher's voice. How did Lauren deal with it, day after day? he wondered. Dale wasn't the only old-timer around here who carried a grudge as wide and strong as the Weber River. She must face this kind of thing on a daily basis.

It pissed him off and made him want to shake the other man. Instead, he pasted on a calm smile. "Dale, if you weren't so stubborn, you would admit Lauren is a fine doctor. She'll take care of the girl. You can bet your ranch on it."

The other man made a harrumphing kind of sound but didn't comment as Teresa Hendricks approached. Daniel turned his attention from defending Lauren—something she would probably neither appreciate nor understand—and focused on the business at hand.

"Thanks for coming in on your first night off

in a week," he said to his deputy. "Sorry to do this to you."

"Not a problem. Sounds like you had some excitement."

He spent five minutes briefing her on the case, then suggested she drive the rancher home and take his statement there, where they both could be warm and dry.

"I'm going to follow the ambulance to the hospital and try to interview the vic," he said. "If anything breaks here, you know how to reach me."

The snow seemed to fall heavier and faster as he drove through Parley's Canyon to the Salt Lake Valley. It was more crowded than he would have expected at eleven at night, until he remembered the film festival. This whole part of the state was insane when all the celebs were in town.

By the time he reached the University of Utah Medical Center, his shoulders ached with tension and he was definitely in need of a beer.

At the hospital, he went immediately to the

emergency room and was directed down a hallway, where he quickly spotted Lauren talking to a man Daniel assumed was another doctor, at least judging by the stethoscope around his neck.

The guy was leaning down, and appeared to be hanging on every word Lauren said. He was blond and lean and as chiseled as those movie stars in their two-thousand-dollar ski jackets up the canyon, trying to see and be seen around town.

Daniel immediately hated him.

He took a step down the hallway and knew immediately when Lauren caught sight of him. She straightened abruptly and something flashed in her blue eyes, something murky and confusing. She quickly veiled her expression and it became a mask of stiff politeness.

Just once, he would love the chance to talk to her without the prickly shell she always seemed to whip out from somewhere and put on whenever he was near.

"Sheriff Galvez," she greeted him, her delicate features solemn. "Have you met Kendall Fox? He's the E.R. attending tonight. Kendall, this is Daniel Galvez."

The doctor stuck out his hand and Daniel shook it, though he couldn't escape the impression they were both circling around each other, sizing up the enemy like a couple of hound dogs sniffing after the same bone.

He didn't miss the dismissal in the doctor's eyes and for the second time that night, he had to fight the urge to kick somebody's ass. He wouldn't waste his energy, he thought. Lauren was too smart to go for the type of smooth player who couldn't remember the name of the woman he was with unless she had it tattooed somewhere on a conveniently accessible portion of her anatomy.

"How's our victim?" he asked.

"She's gone to Radiology for some X-rays," Lauren spoke up. "The tech should be bringing her back in a moment. Kendall…Dr. Fox…

and I were just discussing the best course of action. We think—"

Dr. Jerk cut her off. "She has a little frostbite on a couple of her toes, an apparent broken wrist and some cracked ribs."

"How's the baby?" Daniel pointedly directed his question back to Lauren, ignoring the other man.

She frowned, looking worried. "She's started having some mild contractions right now. We've given her medication to stop them, but she's definitely going to need to be closely observed for the next few days."

"She give any indication who put her here?"

Lauren shook her head. She had discarded her parka somewhere, he observed with his keen detective eye, and had put surgical scrubs on over the pale blue turtleneck she had worn when she treated his shoulder. Her hair was slipping from its braid and he had to fight a ridiculous urge to tuck it back.

"She clams up every time we ask."

"I was afraid of that. She's got to be frightened. It would sure make my job easier if she could just give me the name, age and last-known address of the son of a bitch who put her here. Of course we have to do this the hard way. Can I talk to her?"

"You cops. Can't you even wait until the girl gets out of X-ray?" Fox asked.

Daniel slid his fists into his pockets and pasted on that same damn calm smile that sometimes felt about as genuine as fool's gold.

He really hated being made to feel like a big, dumb Mexican.

"I didn't mean this instant," he murmured. "But I would like to talk to her as soon as possible, while the details are still fresh in her mind."

The doctor looked like he wanted to get in a pissing match right there in the hallway, but before he could unzip, a nurse in pink scrubs stuck her head out of one of the examination rooms.

She didn't look pleased to find the E.R.

doctor still standing close to Lauren, a sentiment with which Daniel heartily concurred. Her reaction made him wonder if the good doctor was the sort who left a swath of broken hearts through the staff.

"Dr. Fox, can you come in here for a minute?" the nurse asked. "I've got a question on your orders."

The doctor's handsome features twisted with annoyance but he hid it well. "Be right there."

After he walked down the hall, a tight, awkward silence stretched between Daniel and Lauren. He found it both sad and frustrating, and wondered how he could ever bridge the chasm between them.

He wasn't exactly sure how much Lauren knew about the events that led up to her father's exposure and subsequent fall from grace. If she knew all of it, she must blame him for what happened next.

He sure as hell blamed himself.

"How's your arm?" she asked.

The blasted thing throbbed like the devil, but he wasn't about to admit that to her.

"Fine," he assured her. "Sorry I wasted your time on that. If I'd known I would have to make a trip down here to the city, I could have just had them fix me up here while I was waiting to interview our beating victim. But then, I doubt anybody on staff here can claim such nice handiwork."

She blinked at the compliment and he watched a light sprinkle of color wash over her cheekbones. "I…thank you," she murmured.

"You're welcome."

They lapsed into silence again.

"How's Anna these days?" Lauren asked after an awkward moment. "I heard she was in the Northwest now."

Grateful for the conversation starter, he smiled at the thought of his baby sister. "She loves Oregon. She runs a little gift shop and gallery in Cannon Beach that seems to be doing well. I took a few days and drove up there last year and she seems happy."

"She's not married?"

Some of the tension between them seemed to ease as they talked and he wanted to prolong the moment indefinitely. "No. Marc's the only one of us to bite the bullet so far. He and his wife live in Cache Valley. They have twin boys we all spoil like crazy."

"And Ren is still in Central America?"

"Right. We can't get him away from his sea turtles."

She opened her mouth to answer, but cut off the words as a hospital worker pushed a gurney around the corner.

"Here's Rosa," she said.

The beating victim looked even younger here in the harsh glare of the hospital lights and her bruises showed up in stark relief against the white linens. Daniel studied her features, trying hard to find any hint of familiarity, but he was certain he didn't know her.

He helped push the gurney through the door into the examination room, earning a censorious look from Lauren for the mild exertion. He returned it with a bland smile, though he had to fight down a spurt of warmth. He liked her worrying about him far too much.

"How did it go, Riley?" she asked the kid, who looked young for an X-ray technician, as his hospital ID identified him.

"Good. She fell asleep while I was waiting for the films and I didn't have the heart to wake her. Poor thing."

"She's been through a terrible ordeal. She must be exhausted."

Lauren took the films from him and slid the first of several into the light box hanging on the wall. She studied it, then exchanged it for another and finally a third, a frown of concentration on her lovely features.

"Just as we suspected," she said after a moment. "She's got three broken ribs, a fractured ulna and a broken nose."

"Somebody did a real number on her." He was angry all over again at the viciousness behind the attack. "How's the baby?"

Lauren studied tape spitting out from a machine that was attached to a belt around Rosa's abdomen. "The contractions have stopped. That's a good sign. We did an ultrasound earlier and the fetus seemed healthy. It's a miracle. She's a dozen different shades of black and blue on her abdomen. My guess is somebody kicked her hard at least two or three times in an effort to induce abortion."

Daniel had a feeling this was one of those cases that would grab on to him with rottweiler jaws and not let go until he solved it. "Can I talk to her?" he asked.

Lauren pursed her lips. "My instincts say to let her sleep for a while, but I understand your urgency. You likely have to return to Moose Springs as soon as possible."

"I do. I'm sorry. We're shorthanded tonight." He paused and met Lauren's gaze. "It's not just

that, though. I want her to tell me what happened.
The quicker she identifies whoever did this to
her, the quicker I can lock the bastard up."

Though he spoke with a hard determination
that didn't bode well for the perpetrator,
Lauren didn't feel so much as a twinge of
sympathy for whoever had done this. They
deserved to feel the full wrath of Daniel
Galvez, a terrible thing indeed.

"I'm right there with you on that sentiment,"
she told him. "In fact, if you gave me half a
chance, I'd like to be the one twisting the key
in the lock."

"I've got to catch him first and I can't do that
until I talk to Rosa."

Lauren sighed. "All right. Why don't you wait
in the hall while I wake her, though. She might
panic if you're the first thing she sees when she
opens her eyes."

He raised an eyebrow. "Am I really that scary?"

She felt her face heat and regretted her fair

coloring that showed every emotion to the world like a big neon billboard. "I meant your uniform," she answered stiffly, though she had to admit, she found the man absolutely terrifying.

Could he tell? she wondered, hoping it wasn't as obvious as her blush. She wasn't afraid he would physically hurt her, though he was big and powerful and all large men tended to make her uncomfortable on some instinctive level.

With Daniel, though, she was more wary of her own reaction to him and all the feelings he sparked in her, emotions she would rather not be experiencing for someone with whom she had such a tangled, complicated relationship.

To her relief, he let the matter drop. "Yell when it's safe for me to come in, then," he murmured, slipping out of the room with far more grace than a man his size should possess.

The room immediately felt about three times bigger without his overwhelming presence filling it. Lauren let out the breath she always seemed to hold around him and moved to her patient's bedside.

"Rosa? *Niña,* I need you to wake up."

When she didn't respond immediately, Lauren gently shook her shoulder. "Rosa?"

The girl's eyes blinked open and she looked around in wild confusion, panic blooming in her dark eyes. Her gaze shifted to Lauren and a light of recognition sparked there. "*Doctora.*" She covered her abdomen with her hands. "*El bebé. Está bien?*"

"*Sí. Sí. Está bien.*" She smiled, wishing she had a little better command of Spanish. If things weren't so tensely uncomfortable with Daniel, she might ask for private lessons. But of course, that was impossible, so for now she would have to muddle through.

"Rosa, the sheriff is here to talk to you about who hurt you."

The panic returned to her features. "*No. No policía.*"

Lauren sighed. The physician in her wanted to

urge her patient to rest, to promise her she could have this difficult interview later when her body had a chance to begin the healing process.

She couldn't, though. Daniel had a job to do—a job she very much wanted to see him conclude with an arrest. She just had to trust that he would handle a frightened girl with both tact and compassion.

"I'm sorry, Rosa," she answered in Spanish. "But you must tell him what happened."

The girl shook her head, her hands clasped protectively around her abdomen as if she feared Daniel would snatch the child from her womb. Lauren gave her a reassuring pat. "It will all be all right. You'll see. Sheriff Galvez only wants to help you."

Rosa said something in Spanish too rapid for Lauren to pick up on. She had a feeling she was better off not knowing.

She went to the door and opened it for Daniel. "She's upset and doesn't want to talk to you," she said in an undertone. "I honestly don't know how much she'll tell you. I'm sorry. I can give you a few moments but if I think you're upsetting her too much, I'll have to kick you out."

"All right."

When he entered the room, Rosa shrank against the bed linens, her fine-boned features tight with tension. Daniel pulled out one of the guest chairs and sat on the edge of it. He moved slowly, like someone trying to coax a meadowlark to eat birdseed from his hand.

He spoke Spanish in a low, calm voice. She couldn't understand him well, both because he pitched his voice low and because he spoke too quickly for her limited comprehension skills.

After a moment, Rosa answered him quickly, reluctance in every line of her body.

Lauren found it a surreal experience trying to follow their conversation when she only understood about one word in five. Even without a perfect command of the language, she could hear the compassion ringing through his voice.

He genuinely cared about Rosa, Lauren thought. The girl might be just a stowaway he had never seen until an hour ago, but he wanted to get to the bottom of things. She suddenly knew Daniel would go to any lengths to protect the girl. Fate had dropped her into Moose Springs, and she had become one of his charges.

She had a feeling his sincerity wasn't translating for Rosa. She shook her head vehemently several times, and Lauren could at least understand the most frequent word the girl employed. "No" sounded the same in English and in Spanish.

After several moments of this, Rosa turned her head against the wall, a clear message that she was done talking to him. Daniel said something, his voice low and intense, but Rosa didn't turn around.

At last Daniel stood with a sigh, his big handsome features tight with frustration. He tucked a business card in Rosa's hand. The girl closed her fingers around it, but didn't even look at either the card or at Daniel. With another sigh, Daniel nodded to Lauren and left the room.

She followed him. "She won't talk?" she asked when the door closed behind them.

"She claims she doesn't remember what happened to her."

Lauren frowned. "She has no head injury that might account for a loss of memory. I suppose it might be some self-protective psychological reaction to the trauma…"

"There *is* no loss of memory. She remembers perfectly. She's just not telling."

"Doesn't she understand her safety and that of her baby is at stake here?"

"I think that's exactly what she's thinking about. I think she just wants to pretend none of it happened. 'I'm fine, the baby's fine. That's all that matters,' she just kept saying over and over."

"I'll talk to her. She'll be under my care and the attending's here for at least the next two or three days. I want to consult with the high-risk ob-gyns on staff here and make sure we monitor her closely to ensure no lasting harm to the fetus from her injuries. I don't know that it will do any good, but I'll try to persuade her she has to talk to you, or whoever did this to her will get away with a double attempted murder."

"Thanks, Lauren. I'll try to stop back in first thing in the morning. Maybe she'll change her mind about talking to me by then."

"You put in long hours, Sheriff."

He smiled and the sight of those white teeth flashing in that darkly handsome face sent her stomach trembling. "I could say the same for you, Doc."

She gazed at him for far longer than was probably polite, until he finally cleared his throat.

"You still need a ride back to Moose Springs?"

Chill, she chided herself. This was Daniel Galvez, the one man in town who shouldn't rev her motor. She would be better off with a player like Kendall Fox. At least he just annoyed her. Being with Dr. Fox never left her feeling like she had just stood in a wind tunnel for two or three days.

"If it's not too much trouble."

"No trouble," he assured her, though she couldn't help feeling he wasn't being completely truthful.

"Just give me a few more moments to wrap things up with Kendall and I should be ready."

"Here comes the good doctor now."

She turned and found Kendall walking purposefully down the hallway.

"The sheriff is my ride back to Moose Springs since I came in the ambulance," she said quickly, hoping to deflect any more flirtation. "Do you mind if I leave my patient in your care?"

"We'll take good care of her until they can find a bed for her on the medical floor."

"I'll be back first thing in the morning to check on her," she said. "I want a phone call in the night if her condition changes at all. Make sure the nurses know that when they admit her upstairs. Any change at all, I want to hear about it."

"I'll take care of her, I promise." Kendall gave her the full wattage of his lady-killer smile. "I'm on until seven in the morning and I expect dough-nuts and some decent coffee out of the deal."

"Done."

As her interactions with Dr. Fox went, this one was fairly innocuous. She could only hope she would get through the hour-long drive with Daniel Galvez as painlessly.

Chapter 3

The slushy snow of earlier in the evening had given way to giant, soft flakes as the temperature dropped. Daniel drove away from the U. toward the canyon that would take them back to Moose Springs through the feeder streets along the foothills. Roads here were mostly clear, though he knew the canyon would probably be dicey.

He was painfully aware of Lauren sitting beside him and wondered if they had ever been alone like this. He was so conscious of her that it took all his powers of concentration to keep his attention on driving as he took the exit to I-80 through the canyon.

Still, he was aware of every movement from her side of the SUV. When he caught her covering a yawn, he risked a look at her. "Go ahead and sleep if you need to. I've got a pillow in the back."

"I'm all right. It's been a rather long day. I imagine you know all about those."

"This week, I certainly do." He signaled to change lanes around a car with out-of-state plates going at a crawl through what was just a light layer of snow.

The scanner crackled with static suddenly and he heard radio traffic of somebody in Park City reporting a drunk-and-disorderly patron at one of the popular restaurants on Main Street.

"I'm sure that's not the first one of those they've had this week," Lauren said.

"Yeah, and it won't be the last until Sundance

is over. The detective I spoke to tonight on the way here sounded just a little frazzled."

"Things are busy enough in Park City in the winter with all the skiers. Throw in the film festival and it's a nightmare."

"Have you been to any screenings this year?"

She shrugged. "I don't have a lot of free hours to go to movies. You?"

"No. I caught a few screenings last year but I'm afraid this one is going to pass me by. Too much work."

"We're pathetic, aren't we? Sounds like we both need to get a life outside our jobs."

"I'd love to," he deadpanned, "but who has the time?"

She laughed out loud at that, the low, musical sound filling all the cold corners of his Tahoe. "*We* are pathetic. I was thinking the exact same thing. By the time I finish a twelve-hour shift at the clinic, I'm lucky to find the energy to drive home."

"You need a vacation." He pushed away the

image of her on a white sand beach somewhere, a soft sea breeze ruffling her hair and her muscles loose and relaxed.

"Funny, that seems to be the consensus," she said. "You'll be surprised to find, I'm sure, that I'm actually taking one next week. Coralee and Bruce Jenkins are going on a cruise. Rather than hire a temp to be the office manager for a week, I decided to close the whole clinic and just give everyone the time off. My staff needed a break."

"Good for you!"

"The town got along without any doctor at all for a long time. I'm sure a few days without me will be bearable."

"What are you doing with yourself?"

"I haven't decided yet. Mom's bugging me to come down and visit for a few days. I might. Or I might just stick close to home, try out some new cross-country ski trails, maybe take in a movie or two in Park City."

"I'm sure Dr. Fox would be happy to take you to a screening if you just said the word."

He immediately wished he had just kept that little statement to himself. Out of the corner of his eye, he saw Lauren's eyes widen with surprise. Even from here, he could see color flare on her delicate cheekbones. "Kendall? I don't think so."

He knew he should let it rest but he just couldn't seem to make himself shut up. "Why?" he pressed. "He's good-looking, successful, probably loaded. Seems like a good catch."

"Maybe *you* should date him," she said tartly.

"I'm not the one the good doctor couldn't take his eyes off."

"You're delusional. I'd be happy to refer you to a doctor who can prescribe something for that."

He laughed, but figured he should probably change the subject before he revealed too much, like the attraction he had done his best to hide for more than a decade. Before he could come up with a conversational detour, she beat him to the punch.

"What about you?" she asked. "I heard

rumors of wedding bells a few summers ago when you were dating little Cheryl White."

"She wasn't little," he muttered.

"Not in physical assets, anyway. But wasn't she barely out of high school?"

He had to admit, he was a little stung by her implication that he might be interested in jailbait. At the same time, he had to wonder why she noticed who he dated. "Cheryl was twenty-one when I started dating her. She didn't even have to use fake ID to get into Mickey's."

"That must have been a relief for you. It probably would have been a little awkward to have to arrest your own girlfriend."

It must be late, if she could tease him like this. The tension usually simmering between them was nowhere in sight as they drove through the snowy night. He savored the moment, though he was fairly certain it wouldn't last.

"For the record, Cheryl was never my girl-friend. We only dated a few times and we never discussed wedding bells or anything else matrimony-related. You ought to know better than to listen to the Moose Springs gossips."

Even without looking at her, he could feel her light mood trickle away like the snow melting on the windshield.

"You're right. Absolutely right." Her voice cooled several degrees in just a few seconds. "Who gossips *to* you will gossip *of* you, isn't that what they say? And I certainly don't need to be the subject of any more whispers in Moose Springs."

The ghost of her father loomed between them and all the usual tension suddenly returned. He would have given anything to take his heedless words back, but like those snippets of gossip spreading around town, they couldn't be recalled.

His hands tightened on the steering wheel and he made some innocuous comment about the weather. She responded in a quiet, polite voice, as if those shared moments of intimacy had never been.

It was nearly midnight when he pulled up in

front of the clinic. Three or four inches of snow had fallen while they had been in the city and her aging Volvo was buried.

He reached across the space between them to his jockey box for his window scraper. The movement brought him closer to her and he was surrounded by jasmine and vanilla.

His mouth watered and his insides gave one big sigh, but he did his best to ignore his automatic reaction. He pulled out the scraper and returned to the safe side of the vehicle—but not before he heard a quick, indrawn breath from Lauren.

He chanced a look at her. The SUV was parked under a lamppost and in the pool of light, he found her blue eyes wide and her lovely features slightly pink.

He wasn't quite sure what to think about that so decided to put it from his mind. "Wait here where it's warm," he ordered.

Her forehead furrowed with her frown and now any flush that might be on her features turned to annoyance. "Are you kidding? I just put seven stitches in your arm, Daniel. *You* wait here where it's warm. Better yet, go on home and rest. I don't need a police escort to scrape the snow off my car."

"Wait here," he repeated, in the same no-nonsense voice he used with the prisoners at the jail.

Her sigh sounded exasperated, but he didn't let that stop him as he stepped out into the blowing cold that soaked through the layers of his coat to settle in his bones.

Nights like this made him feel all his thirty-three years—and more—and he couldn't help but remember every single hit he took as a running back at Wyoming. He ignored the aches, especially the throb and pull of the stitches in his arm, as he brushed the snow off her car then scraped the thick ice underneath.

He wasn't particularly surprised—just annoyed—when she joined him in the cold. She slid into the driver's seat of her vehicle and turned over the engine. After a chugging kind of start, the motor engaged. A moment later, she emerged with another window scraper and went to work on the other side of the vehicle.

When the windows were clear, she stood back. "Thank you for your help," she murmured. "And for the ride."

He didn't want it to end, he realized, as tense and uncomfortable as things became at the end there.

How pathetic was that?

"Don't you have any gloves?" he asked. "Your hands are going to be freezing by the time you get home."

"They're around somewhere. I keep buying pairs and losing them between here and my house."

He reached into the pocket of his parka. "Here. Take mine. I've got an extra pair in the squad vehicle."

Her mouth lifted slightly. "No offense, Sheriff, but your hands are a little bigger than mine." She waggled delicate fingers that would be dwarfed by his gloves and he felt huge and awkward. "Thank you for the offer but it's only half a mile. I should be fine."

"Good night, then," he said. "Thanks again for your help earlier stitching me up."

"You're welcome. Be careful of those sutures."

She smiled a little and it took all his will-power to keep from reaching between them, tucking her into his warmth and kissing the tired corner of that mouth.

She climbed into the Volvo and he returned to his Tahoe as she slowly pulled out of the parking lot into the deserted streets, her tires crunching on snow.

He pulled out behind her and they seemed to be the only fools out on the road on a cold January night. Everybody else must be snuggled together at home.

Okay, he didn't need that image in his head. Suddenly the only thing he could think about was cuddling under a big quilt with Lauren in front of a crackling fire while the snow pelted the windows, her soft body wrapped around him and jasmine and vanilla seducing his senses.

Reality was light-years away from fantasy—so far it would have been amusing if he didn't find it so damn depressing as he followed her through the snowy streets.

She lived on the outskirts of town, in a trim little clapboard house set away from her neighbors, the last house before the mountains. When they reached it, Lauren pulled into her garage and slid from her Volvo. In the dim garage light, he could clearly see her exasperated look as she waved him on.

He shook his head and gestured to the house. He waited until the lights came on inside and the garage door closed completely before he drove off into the snowy night.

She stood at her living room window watching Daniel's big SUV cruise slowly down the street. How very like him to follow her home simply to ensure she made it in safely. It wasn't necessary. The distance between the clinic and her house wasn't far. Even if her ancient car sputtered and gave out on the way, she could easily walk home—in good weather, she walked to and from work all the time.

Yet Daniel had been concerned enough to take time out of his busy schedule to follow her home. A slow, steady warmth spread out from her core as she watched his taillights disappear in the snow.

She shouldn't feel so warm and comforted by his simple gesture, as if those big, strong arms were wrapped around her. It was foolish to be so touched, but she couldn't remember the last time someone had fussed over her with such concern.

Just his nature, she reminded herself. Daniel was a caretaker. He always had been. She could remember watching him on the bus with his three younger siblings, how he had always stood between them and anybody who might want to bully them. He wouldn't let anybody push them around, and nobody dared. Not if they had to run the risk of incurring the wrath of big Danny Galvez.

Oh, she had envied them. His sister had been in her grade and Lauren used to be so jealous that Anna had an older brother to watch out for her. Two of them, since Ren was just a year younger than Daniel.

She had longed for a noisy, happy family like the Galvezes. For siblings to fight and bicker and share with.

Siblings. Her mouth tightened and she let the curtain fall, hating the word. She shouldn't feel this anger at her father all over again but she couldn't seem to help herself.

She had siblings as well. Three younger brothers from her father's second family, the one she and her mother had known nothing about until after R.J.'s suicide and all her father's dark secrets came to light.

A few years ago she had met them and their mother—a woman who had been as much in the dark about her husband's other life and Lauren and her mother as they had been about her. They had all seemed perfectly nice. Children who had adored R.J. as much as she had and a widow who had still seemed shell-shocked.

They hadn't wanted any further relationship. Just as well, because Lauren didn't know if she quite had the stomach to continue being polite to the innocent children who had been the cause of R.J.'s relentless need for cash. Maintaining two households couldn't have been cheap and her father's way of augmenting his income was dipping into the public till.

She sighed and pushed thoughts of her half siblings away, focusing instead on Daniel Galvez and his caretaking of the world.

She shouldn't feel singled out simply because he followed her home to make sure she arrived safely. This wasn't any kind of special treatment, just Daniel's way with everyone.

Imagining it meant anything other than politeness would be a dangerous mistake.

She turned away from the window and the dark night. Returning to her empty house late at night always depressed her, highlighting the lonely corners of her life. She needed a dog, a big friendly mutt to lick her chin and rub against her legs and curl up at her feet on the rare evenings she was home.

With her insane hours, she knew that wouldn't be fair to any living creature, though perhaps she should get a fish or something, just for the company.

She turned on the television for noise and headed for the bathroom. A good, long soak in hot water would chase away the tension of the day and perhaps lift her spirits.

She had no reason to be depressed. She was doing the job she loved, the one she had dreamed of since she was a young girl in junior high biology class. If she had no one to share it all with, that was her own fault.

She was lonely. That was the long and short of it. She longed for someone to talk to at the end of the day, for a warm body to hold on a winter's night.

Too bad her options were so limited here—eligible single males weren't exactly thick on the ground in a small town like Moose Springs—but she was determined to stay here, come hell or high water.

What other choice did she have? She owed the town a debt she could never fully repay, though she tried her best. She couldn't in good conscience move away somewhere more lucrative and leave behind the mess her father had created.

The best cure for loneliness was hard work and she had never shied away from that. And perhaps she ought to stay away from Daniel, since spending any time at all with him only seemed to accentuate all the things missing in her life.

Her gray mood had blown away with the storm as she drove through the predawn darkness the next day through town. Her clinic hours started at nine but she figured if she left early enough, she could make it to see Rosa at the hospital in Salt Lake City and be back before the first patient walked through the door.

She felt energized for the day ahead as she listened to *Morning Edition* on NPR. The morning was cold and still, the snow of the night before muffling every sound. She waved at a few early-morning snow-shovelers trying to clear their driveways before heading to work.

Most of them waved back as she passed, but a few quite noticeably turned their backs on her. She sighed but decided not to let it ruin her good mood.

This area was settled by pioneer farmers and ranchers and for years they had made up the bedrock of the rural economy. But for the last decade or so Moose Springs had become more of a bedroom community to workers in Park City and Salt Lake City who were looking for a quiet, mostly safe place to raise their families.

She was glad to see newcomers in town and figured an infusion of fresh blood couldn't hurt. Still, she hoped this area was able to hang on to all the small-town things she had always loved about it.

The interstate through the canyon was busy with morning commuters heading into the city, but the snow had been cleared in the night so the drive was pleasant.

As she had promised, she stopped at her favorite bakery not far from the hospital to pick up a dozen doughnuts and several cups of coffee for Kendall and the floor nurses.

Juggling the bag, the cup holder and her laptop, she hurried inside the hospital and went straight for the E.R., hoping she could catch the nurses who had helped with Rosa before their shift changed in a half hour. She had learned early in her career that nurses were the heart and soul of a hospital and she always tried to go out of her way to let them know how much she appreciated their hard work.

She found several nurses gathered at the station. They greeted her with friendly smiles.

"No sexy sheriff with you this morning?" Janie Carpenter, one of the nurses she had worked with before, asked her.

If only. She shook her head. "Sorry. I'm on my own. But I brought goodies, if that helps."

"I don't know." A round, middle-aged nurse grinned. "Between doughnuts or a hottie like that, I'd choose the sheriff every time. I was thinking I just might have to drive to Moose Springs and rob a bank or something. I certainly wouldn't mind that man putting me under arrest."

"Or under anything else," Janie purred. "Think he might use handcuffs?"

Lauren could feel herself blush. She wanted to tell them Daniel was far more than just chiseled features and strong, athletic shoulders. But maybe he enjoyed being drooled over. She pulled one of the doughnuts out and grabbed the last cup of coffee in the drink holder.

"I owe this to Dr. Fox. Is he around?"

Janie rolled her eyes. "Haven't seen him for a while. He's probably flirting with the nurses on the surgical floor. I'll be happy to set it aside for him, though."

She handed over the stash, not believing her for a second. Oh, well, she tried. It was Kendall's own fault for being such a player.

She waved goodbye to the nurses and headed up to Rosa's floor. Nobody was in sight at the nurse's station on this floor except a dour-looking maintenance man haphazardly swirling a mop around.

Served her right for coming just as the nurses were giving report. She could hear them in the lounge as the night shift caught the fresh blood up on their caseload.

She smiled at the janitor but he still didn't meet her eye so she gave up trying to be nice and began looking for Rosa's chart. Probably in with the nurses, she realized, and went to the lounge to ask if they were done with it.

"Here it is. She had a very quiet night," a tired-looking nurse said, handing over the chart. "No more contractions and I peeked in on her about an hour ago and she was sleeping soundly."

"Thank you."

When Lauren returned to the desk, the janitor was gone. She spent a moment flipping through the chart, pleased with what she saw there. Her vitals were stable and her pain level seemed to be under control. The few times she had awakened, she had seemed calm and at ease.

Lauren didn't want to wake her patient, but she also didn't want to leave after coming all this way without at least checking on her.

As she paused outside the door to her room, a strange whimpering noise sounded from inside and her heart sank. Despite what the night nurse had charted, maybe the mild pain-killers Rosa had been treated with weren't quite cutting it.

She pushed open the door to check on the girl, then gasped.

The horrific sight inside registered for only about half a second before Lauren started screaming for security and rushed inside to attack the man who was trying to smother her patient.

Chapter 4

After that first instant of disoriented, stunned panic, everything else seemed a blur. She rushed the man, almost tripping over the mop and bucket on her way toward him as she yelled for him to stop and for security at equal turns.

With no coherent plan, she slammed into him to knock him away from her patient. The force of her movement knocked them both off balance and they toppled against the rolling bedside table, sending it crashing to the floor and the two of them after it.

The man scrambled to his feet to get away and Lauren lunged after him, barely registering the coarse fabric of his janitor's uniform as she grabbed hold of it. For some wild reason she was intent only on keeping him there until security arrived, but he was just as intent on escape.

He shoved her to get her away from him, hissing curses at her in Spanish as he fought her off. Finally he just swung his other beefy fist out and slugged her, the blow connecting to the cheekbone and knocking her to the ground.

White-hot pain exploded in her skull. In an instant he was gone. She couldn't have stopped him, even if she hadn't been forced to release him when she fell.

Lauren's vision grayed and her stomach twisted and heaved from the pain. She wanted to curl up right there on the floor, but Rosa was clutching her throat and still gasping for air. Lauren forced herself to keep it together for her patient's sake. Using the bed for support, she pulled herself to her feet and hurried as fast as possible to the terrified girl's side.

"Come on, sweetheart," Lauren urged, grabbing the oxygen mask from the wall above the bed and placing it as gently as possible over Rosa's mouth at the same time she hit the emergency call button.

"Take deep breaths. That's the way. You're fine now. Nobody's going to hurt you."

Though she forgot all about the language barrier and spoke in English, Rosa seemed to understand her. The shaken girl made a ragged, gravelly sound deep in her throat and Lauren handed her the water glass by the side of her bed just as the first nurses rushed in.

"What is it? What happened?" the first one asked. "Are you okay?"

Lauren was shaking, she realized, and her head throbbed like it had been crushed by a wrecking ball. "No. I'm not okay. A man just attacked my patient. Call security. Have them block all the exits and entrances. They need to look for a Latino male in his mid-twenties. He was wearing a maintenance worker's uniform but it was too short for him so I'm guessing it wasn't real."

"You're bleeding!" the nurse exclaimed.

"Forget about me," she said harshly. "Just call security!"

The nurse rushed out and Rosa gave a strangled whimper. Lauren saw she was inches away from hysteria. She slid onto the bed and gathered the girl to her, as much to comfort her as to find a safe place to sit for a moment before her legs gave out.

"You're okay. You're safe now."

"Mi bebé. Mi bebé."

"Okay, okay. We'll check everything out but I'm sure your baby is all right."

As the adrenaline spike crested, Lauren had to fight to hold on to her meager breakfast. It wasn't easy.

She had been physically attacked only once before in her life and finding herself in this situation again brought back all those long-dormant feelings of shock and invasion she thought she had worked through years ago.

She didn't know what was stronger, the urge to vomit or the urge to crawl into a corner and sob.

"Rosa. Is that the same man who hurt you?"

The girl hesitated, though Lauren could tell she understood her fractured Spanish.

"The only way you can be safe is to report what happened so he can be arrested."

The gross hypocrisy of her words struck her, but she couldn't worry about that now. Not when her patient's life was at stake.

"Rosa, you're going to have to tell someone what happened. You have no choice anymore. Will you talk to Sheriff Galvez?"

Rosa let out a sob and curved both hands over her abdomen. After a moment, she gave a long, slow nod.

He was bone-tired, so tired all he wanted to do was pull over somewhere, put his hat over his face and doze off for a few decades.

A smart man would be home in bed right about now dreaming soft, pleasant dreams that had nothing to do with crimes or accident reports or people in need.

He, on the other hand, had decided on a wild hair to drive into the big city after his shift ended to check on their assault victim. He could only hope a night in the hospital had changed her mind about talking to him about what had happened to her.

He worked out the kinks in his neck as he parked his SUV and headed for the front entrance of the hospital. Four security guards and a Salt Lake City police officer stood just inside, a pretty heavy security force. Maybe they had beefed up security for some kind of high-profile patient. His guess was that some kind of A-list movie star from the film festival had broken a leg on the slopes or something.

He recognized the city cop as Eddie Marin, an old friend from police training. "Hey, Eddie. What's going on?"

The officer greeted him with familiar back-slapping. "Galvez, long time no see."

"What's with all the uniforms?"

"Incident up on the medical unit. Some dude tried to off a patient. We've sealed off the entrances but the guy seems to be in the wind. We can't find any trace of him." He gave Daniel a considering look. "Not saying we don't appreciate all the help we can get, but isn't this one a little far out of your jurisdiction?"

"I'm off duty, just following up on an assault victim dumped in my neck of the woods. What does your suspect look like? I'll keep an eye out for him on my way up."

"We had an eyewitness who caught him in the attack and was hurt trying to fight him off. She was pretty shaken up but Dr. Maxwell described a Latino male in a janitor uniform, five feet eleven inches, one hundred ninety pounds, half his left eyebrow missing from a scar. Only problem is, we can't find the bastard anywhere in the hospital."

Daniel registered none of the description, too caught up in the words preceding it. "Did you say Dr. Maxwell? Lauren Maxwell?"

"I think that's her name. You know her?"

"She was injured?"

Eddie blinked at his urgent tone. "Perp punched her and knocked her to the floor. She's pretty banged up and needs a couple stitches but she won't leave her patient."

"What room?"

Eddie gave him a careful look. "You okay, man?"

"What the hell room are they in?"

The officer told him and Daniel didn't bother waiting for the elevator, he just raced for the stairs, his heart pounding.

He wouldn't say he was intimately familiar with the sprawling hospital but he had been here many times on other cases. He knew his way enough to find the room Eddie had indicated, and in moments he reached the medical wing.

Even if the officer hadn't given him the room

number, he would have known it instantly by the crowd of people milling around. His own uniform seemed to smooth the way as he fought his way through until he made it to the room.

He found Lauren just outside the doorway, gesturing to another Salt Lake police officer he didn't recognize.

She was holding a blood-soaked bandage to her cheek and her face was pale and drawn. Rage burned through him at whatever bastard might have hurt her and he wanted to fold her against him and keep her safe from the world.

She cut off her words the moment she saw him.

"Daniel!" she exclaimed, shock and relief mingling in her voice. Before he quite knew how it happened, she seemed to slide into his arms, pressing her uninjured cheek against the fabric of his uniform and holding on tight.

She felt delicate and fragile against him and despite the layers of his coat, he could feel the tiny shudders that shook her frame.

She sagged against him for only a moment,

just long enough for him to want to tighten his arms and hold on forever. After entirely too short a time, she pulled away, a rosy flush replacing the pale, washed-out look she had worn when he first saw her.

He wanted to pull her back into his arms but he knew they didn't have that kind of relationship. The only reason she had turned to him in the first place was likely because he represented a familiar face, comfort and security amid her trauma.

Already, he could see her replacing the defenses between them and once more becoming the cool, controlled physician who could handle anything.

"What happened?" he asked.

She let out a breath. "It was terrible. Absolutely awful. I walked into the room to check on Rosa about half an hour ago and found a janitor with his hands around her neck, choking the life out of her. Only he obviously wasn't really a janitor. She says he was the same one who attacked her."

"How is she?"

Her eyes softened and he had the impression that had been exactly the right thing to say, though he wasn't quite sure why.

"Petrified and shocked. She keeps saying *mi bebé* over and over. Physically, I don't think she was injured by the latest attack but she's severely traumatized by it."

"And you?"

"I'm all right. He got in a good punch. I tried to hold him until security got here but he…he was bigger and stronger than I was."

Her shoulders trembled again. To hell with this, he thought, and pulled her back into his arms, whether she wanted to be there or not. He didn't know if the move was for her comfort or his own, he only knew he couldn't let her stand inches away from him and suffer.

This time she stayed a little longer before she slid away from him. "I'm okay. I am. A little shaky but I'll be fine. I'm glad you're here."

He knew she meant on a professional level, but the words warmed him anyway. He was grateful to be there, too, and had to wonder what higher power had inspired him to drive to the hospital this morning, exactly when he would be needed.

If he hadn't stopped for coffee on the way, though, he might have made it in time to stop the bastard. The thought haunted him.

"Do you think after this latest attack, Rosa might be ready to tell us what's going on?"

Lauren sighed heavily. "I think she's realizing she doesn't have any other choice if she wants to stay alive. I asked her and she agreed she would talk to you."

He didn't want to leave Lauren, but a nurse approached them. "Dr. Maxwell, the surgeon is ready for you."

"Surgeon?" he exclaimed.

She made a face, then winced at the motion. "Plastic surgeon. It's stupid but the hospital insisted he be the one to stitch up my cheek."

"Careful of the needles. I hate those things."

She gave him a half smile, which was all she

seemed to be able to manage with her battle scars. "How can a man who played football against three-hundred-pound linebackers be afraid of a tiny needle?"

"What can I say? I'm a wimp."

She smiled again, looking noticeably more calm than she had when he arrived.

"Go take care of your face," he urged. "I'll go see if I can persuade Rosa to talk to me."

When he walked into the hospital room this time, Rosa didn't look surprised or frightened to see him, only resigned. Such fatalism in features as young and battered as hers was disconcerting.

He greeted her in Spanish. "How are you feeling?" he asked.

"Like I've been kicked by twenty donkeys," she answered quietly.

He met her gaze intently. "You have to tell me what is going on, Rosa. You know that, don't you?"

One hand was in a cast, but the other fingers

tightened on the blanket and she suddenly seemed painfully young. "I am afraid."

"I understand that. Anyone in your position would be. But we can't help you unless we know who is trying to hurt you and your baby."

She closed her eyes, one hand resting on her abdomen. When she opened her eyes again, the raw fear in them twisted his heart.

"Rosa?" he prompted.

She sighed as if the entire weight of the world rested on her narrow shoulders. "His name is Gilberto Mata."

"Is he your baby's father?"

She looked down at the tiny mound beneath the covers. A spasm of emotion that almost looked like shame tightened her mouth. "I don't know. Maybe. It could be him or... others."

Her lip trembled and she wouldn't meet his gaze. He had to wonder if she might feel more comfortable with a female investigator, but he didn't want to interrupt the flow of her story by asking her, not when she seemed willing to tell him what had happened.

"Is that why he hurt you?" Daniel asked. "Because you had been with other men?"

She gave a harsh laugh and this time she did look at him, a deep, horrible bitterness in her eyes. "No. He was there when I was with the other men. He stood by laughing while all three of them, they raped me. And then he took his turn."

Madre de Dios. What the hell kind of trouble was this little girl mixed up with? He fought the urge to squeeze her hand and tell her everything would be all right.

"I am so sorry, Rosa," he finally said, abashed at the inadequacy of the words. "Maybe you had better start at the beginning."

She wiped away a single tear. "The beginning seems another lifetime ago. Six months ago I was working in Tegucigalpa. My mama, she died two years ago. I tried to stay in our village but there was no work and I had no money. I went to the city with my friend Consuela and we found work in a factory sewing clothes."

"How old are you?"

"I will be sixteen years on July sixth," she said, looking a little surprised by the question.

Daniel tried to put the years together. If her mother had died two years ago, she would have been about fourteen when she took a factory job.

"Consuela and I, we did not make much money but it was good, honest work. One day some men came to the factory. They talked to some of the girls and said we could find work in America and they would help us. They filled our stupid heads with stories of the riches we would find here and the good life we would have, like in the movies we see. I did not believe them, but Consuela, she wanted to try. The men flattered her, told her she was beautiful, that she would find good work. I tried to talk her out of it but she would not listen. She begged me to go with her and I finally agreed.

I just wanted to protect her, and without her I had no one left in my country."

She bunched the blanket in her uncasted hand. "For five days Consuela and I and a dozen other girls rode in the back of a closed truck, with no food and only a little water. It was so hot and we thought we would die. At last we arrived in Texas but for some of us, our journey was not done. They told us they had good work for us in Utah. Stupid fools, we believed them."

Another tear trickled down her cheek and he handed her a tissue from a box by the bed. "What happened when you got here?"

"I soon realized what kind of work we were to do. Prostitutes. Whores. They told us if we did not do what they wanted, we would be killed. I would not do it. I was a good girl in Honduras. So the bosses, the men who brought us here…they forced me. Gilberto, he is the worst. We were all afraid of him."

Daniel clamped down his fury, doing his best

to hide it so he wouldn't frighten Rosa. He couldn't conceive the kind of animals who would force young, innocent girls into a dark, ugly world of prostitution. That such things were happening only miles from his safe, quiet town seemed an abomination.

"I was lucky. Because I cried so much when…when they made me do those things, I only had to wash the dishes, do the laundry and scrub the floors."

"Do you know where this all happened?"

"Six of us work above a bar in the town of Park City. The Lucky Strike. The others, including my friend Consuela, are in Salt Lake City somewhere. I do not know where."

"What happened to make Gilberto want to hurt you?"

"It was my fault. A few months ago I discovered I was pregnant from…from that first week. I was angry at first and hated what was inside me as much as I hated whatever man had put the baby inside me. But after some time, I knew

I couldn't blame the baby, that nothing was her fault. I tried to hide it and find a way to escape. They watch us carefully and lock us in at night but I thought I might be able to sneak out the window. I didn't know where I would go after that but I knew I must get away. They would kill my baby. They had made one of the other girls have an abortion and I knew they would do the same to me."

She shivered. "Last night I tried to escape but Gilberto, he found me. He…he beat me and was going to rape me again. Then he saw I was pregnant and he started calling me names, hitting and kicking me, trying to make me lose the baby, too. I fought him and knocked him down the stairs, then ran as fast as I could. It was a big crowd on the street and somehow I got away from him. I ran and ran until I had no more breath. I thought I would die, I hurt so much. I didn't know what to do, then I saw a truck parked in front of me. I could see a blanket inside, and the back, it was unlocked. I climbed inside and pulled the blanket over my head to hide from Gilberto. The next I remember, the man with the white hair opened the truck and found me there. And that is all."

An understatement if he ever heard one. Human smuggling, rape, forced prostitution, attempted murder. There were more class-A felonies in this girl's story than he sometimes dealt with in six months.

"I thought I was safe now, until I woke up in the hospital and found Gilberto in my hospital room. Again, I expected to die and then the pretty doctor, she came rushing in and fought him off."

She sniffled a little and he handed her another tissue. "I am sorry she was hurt. I did not believe Gilberto would find me here."

"That's a good point. How *did* he find you? Did you call someone and tell them you were in the hospital?"

"No. No one. Who would I call? I told you, my friend Consuela, I do not know how to reach her now. They separated us and she is working in Salt Lake City. The other girls at the bar, we did not talk much. They kept us apart most of the time. I know no one else."

It didn't make sense. He supposed they could have been monitoring police traffic on a scanner when they had called for an ambulance to transport her here. It was the only explanation he could come up with, though it seemed a stretch.

"Why does Gilberto want you dead badly enough to come here and try to finish the job?"

"Because I am a fool." She wiped at her eyes again. "Do you know what it is like to be afraid and filled with anger at the same time? When Gilberto was hurting me and…and trying to hurt the baby, I…I told him to stop, that if he did not, I would go to the police, I would tell them everything that had happened to us here since we left Honduras. I had more freedom than the other girls because I cleaned the rooms. I do not snoop, but I see things and I knew the names of the men who hurt me and who made the other girls do those things."

"Everyone?"

"Except the big boss. I do not know his name and I have not seen him, I only know he is Anglo. But I lied. I told Gilberto I did. I should not have said that but I only wanted him to stop hitting me. I thought if he was afraid of being arrested he would let me go."

She covered her face. "I was stupid. An imbecile. He only hit me harder and I knew he would kill me."

"You can't blame yourself, *niña*. None of this is your fault."

She started to weep then, huge, wrenching sobs, and Daniel leaned forward and squeezed her shoulder. The next moment, she threw herself against him, sniffling against his uniform in much the same place Lauren had done.

He patted her hair awkwardly, wishing he had some words that might make this miserable situation all better. Before he could come up with anything, the door opened and Lauren came in. She paused in the doorway, a soft, arrested look in her eyes he didn't quite understand.

She had a stark white bandage on her cheek, but the color had returned to her features, he was grateful to see.

"I'm sorry to interrupt, but Rosa is overdue for pain medication and I don't want her to get behind. How are you?" The last words were in Spanish, directed at the girl.

"Better," Rosa said shyly. She laid back against the pillow, her gaze on Lauren's bandage. "I am sorry you were hurt by Gilberto Mata. He is a bad, bad man and would have killed me if not for you. You saved my life."

Lauren blinked a little at her gratitude, then smiled. "Daniel, will you tell her I didn't go to all the trouble to fix her up only to lose her again to this Mata character?"

Daniel complied.

"How long will I stay here?" Rosa asked.

"I can't answer that right now," Lauren said, and Daniel translated for her. "At least tonight,

I'm thinking. They're going to move you to a more secure location in the hospital."

"Are you leaving?" Daniel asked.

"My clinic is supposed to be opening—" she checked her watch "—right now. I can reschedule some of my patients but not all of them. Tell Rosa I'll be back later this afternoon after I'm through at the clinic."

Rosa yawned suddenly and Daniel thought she must be exhausted after her ordeal of the morning and by the retelling of her story.

Lauren picked up on it as well. "Get some rest. They should be moving you sometime this morning, but rest until then." She paused. "Sheriff Galvez, may I have a word with you?"

Curious, he nodded and followed her from the room.

"Did she tell you what this is all about?"

He nodded. "She and several other girls have been smuggled out of Central America to be used as prostitutes and unpaid labor."

"Slavery?" She looked appalled.

"It's alive and well in the underground," he said. "And a much bigger problem than many people realize. Rosa tried to escape when she realized she was pregnant as a result of rape in her early days in the country. She was caught and beaten because of what she knows and because she threatened to go to the police. I don't think they'll stop with one attempt on her life, especially now that they know for sure she's here."

"We can't leave her here unprotected with some maniac on the loose. I've talked to the hospital and they're going to put full-time security outside her room but I'm not sure some rent-a-cop will be enough. What else can be done?"

"I'll make sure there is adequate protection. You do realize, this is bigger than the Moose Springs Sheriff Department can handle. I'm going to have to call in the FBI on this one and I'm sure they'll set up a multijurisdictional task force."

"Good. I hope they find the bastards who did this to her and string them up by their *cojones*."

He blinked at such fierceness coming from the cool, collected Dr. Maxwell. But then he looked at the bandage marring the soft loveliness of her features and couldn't help but agree.

Chapter 5

Lauren was an hour and a half late for her first appointment of the day and spent most of the morning trying her best to catch up without sacrificing the personalized time she liked to spend with each patient—all while her mind seemed stuck on a courageous young girl recovering in a hospital miles away.

One of the things she enjoyed most about being a small-town doctor was the sheer variety of patients she saw, everything from prenatal visits to setting broken arms to pulling slivers out of tiny fingers. Every day was different, full of new challenges to test her abilities.

Just now she was seeing one of her favorite patients, Cameron Vance. Cam had epilepsy and though he regularly saw a neurologist at the children's hospital in Salt Lake City, she was still his primary care provider and saw him for routine visits.

Just now he was suffering from a case of the sniffles that had lasted for ten days.

"Besides the gross runny nose, how's everything else going with my favorite climber dude?" she asked him.

Cameron grinned. "Awesome. Me and Cale are gonna go to Jackson Hole and climb the Grand Teton this summer. We're in training."

At that surprising bit of information, Lauren raised an eyebrow to his mother, Megan, one of her good friends.

Megan shrugged. "What can I do?" she said. "Cale assures me Cameron has the climbing skills to handle it. He'll be ten by then and is certainly experienced enough for it. I can't really say no, especially since he hasn't had a seizure since the big one last summer."

Lauren knew just which *big one* Megan referred to. In August, Cameron had been lost in an abandoned mine in the foothills above Moose Springs and had gone without his seizure medication for more than thirty-six hours. He had been rescued in the middle of a prolonged grand mal seizure by Cale Davis, one of the FBI agents assigned to his case, just seconds before a mine cave-in would have trapped them all.

At Christmastime, Megan had married the man who had rescued her son and Lauren was thrilled to see them all so happy.

"Cale will take care of him," she assured Megan now. "He won't take Cameron anywhere it's not safe. He's a great stepdad."

"He is, isn't he?" Megan glowed when she talked about her husband and, as happy as she was for her friend, Lauren couldn't help the little spurt of envy.

It was small of her, she knew. Megan hadn't had an easy time of things. Cam and his sister, Hailey, had lost their father a few years ago when he was killed fighting in Afghanistan. Megan had raised her children alone, dealing with all the emotional and physical strain of Cameron's epilepsy. She deserved every slice of happiness she could find and Caleb Davis was a great guy who was obviously crazy about her.

Lauren was thrilled for her. But in comparison to Megan's newfound joy, her own personal life fell somewhere between dry and excruciatingly dull.

"What do you recommend for Cam?" Megan asked now and Lauren jerked her mind away from her own private pity party and focused on her patient, as she should have been doing all along.

"I'm guessing with the duration of his

symptoms, we're looking at a sinus infection here."

"That's what I thought, too."

"You don't need me, do you?" She smiled at Megan.

"Yes, I do," Megan said firmly. "I don't know what we would do without you and your clinic so close."

She might not have a personal life, but she did have a pretty darn good professional one, Lauren reminded herself. "I'm going to write Mr. Monkey here a prescription for an antibiotic that should be fine with his other medications. As to the cold symptoms, I know you're leery about giving him some of the over-the-counter decongestants because of the chance they may trigger a seizure. The best thing I can recommend is some good old-fashioned chicken noodle soup. If you want, I can e-mail my favorite recipe with plenty of garlic and onions. That should help clear him out."

"Definitely. I'm always looking for soup recipes."

She made a note reminding herself to send it as soon as they finished. "If his symptoms don't improve in a couple of days, call me back and we'll try to figure something else out."

"More garlic, maybe?"

Lauren smiled. "It couldn't hurt."

She turned to Cam. "Let me know when you and Cale head off for the big climb. I'm going to want pictures of you on top of the Grand to hang in my office. And let's hope your nose has stopped running by then, because that would just be gross at high altitude."

They shared a grin as Megan took the scribbled prescription from her and stuck it in her purse.

"Thanks, Lauren," she said on her way out the door.

As they were her last appointment before lunch, Lauren walked them out to the waiting room.

Her office manager held up a hand to stop them. "You're probably getting a bit on the old side for a sticker," Coralee said to Cameron. "But can I interest you in a sour ball?"

"Heck, yeah," he exclaimed. At a chiding look from his mother he rolled his eyes. "Yes, ma'am," he corrected. "Thank you."

Coralee grinned and was pulling out her secret stash of candy when the low chime on the door rang. Lauren looked up and was startled to find Daniel standing in the doorway, looking big and tough and intimidating.

To her dismay, her pulse quickened and everything inside her seemed to sigh in welcome.

He looked exhausted, she thought. His eyes were bleary and he needed a shave, and she had to wonder when he had slept last.

"Sheriff Galvez!" Cameron exclaimed and bounded over to Daniel. At the sight of the boy, he straightened and seemed to lock away his exhaustion. The two of them greeted each other with a series of high fives and handshakes that looked as complicated as it was well-choreographed.

"Hey, Cam. Megan. Two of my favorite people. How's everything at the Vance-Davis compound?"

Megan hugged him. "Good. When are you coming to dinner again? You owe us, since you bailed the last time."

"Sorry." He made a rueful face. "That was the night we had that bad accident out on Barrow Road, wasn't it?"

"That time. Before that, it was the structure fire at James Woolstenhume's barn and the time before that was a traffic stop that turned into a drug bust, I think. The next time we invite you to dinner, do me a favor and try to keep the emergencies to a minimum, won't you?"

He smiled with affection at her teasing. "I'll do my best. Can't make any promises."

"That's the trouble with you law enforcement types." Megan nudged his shoulder. His good one, Lauren was relieved to see. "Next week, okay? Which night works for you, Friday or Saturday?"

"Uh, I'll have to check my schedule and get back to you."

"Lauren, you should come, too. I've been meaning to have you out again. We'll make it a party."

Megan gave her a guileless smile, but Lauren could swear she felt the tug of a matchmaking web.

She flushed and didn't dare look at Daniel. "I'm supposed to be on vacation next week."

"Good, then you'll have plenty of time to get ready." Megan didn't wait for an answer as she herded Cameron toward the door. "I'll call you both in a day or two to work out the details. Thanks again for the prescription. Let's hope it takes care of this kiddo's runny nose."

"I…you're welcome."

After the door closed behind him, the room seemed to steady as if they had all just been caught in the eye of a cyclone. She finally risked a look at Daniel and found him looking as nonplussed as she felt. She was about to ask him about Rosa when he turned away from her and headed for the reception desk.

"What's this I hear about you heading out on a cruise, Coralee? When do you sail?"

Lauren's office manager was always eager to talk about her trip. "Next week. I've already got my bags all packed, waiting by the door."

"You'll have to forgive me," Daniel drawled, "but I'm having a real tough time picturing Bruce on the beaches of Tahiti, soaking up the sun in a Speedo."

"Oh, heaven forbid!" Coralee made a face. "He says he's just coming along for the food and the fishing. Though I'm sure he won't mind seeing the island girls in their hula skirts."

"How's Sherry?" he asked, launching Coralee into her second favorite topic after her upcoming vacation—her grandchildren. Lauren stood back and watched them, marveling that he could make small talk with all the heavy matters that must be weighing on his mind.

This was part of the ebb and flow of a small community, stopping and talking and asking after loved ones.

Daniel seemed comfortable talking to everyone in town, which was one of the things that made him such a good sheriff. He was respected and well-liked by all segments of Moose Springs, from kids like Cameron to the low-income families to the town leaders.

He appeared to get along with everybody in town—except her.

She sighed, wishing that thought didn't depress her so much. Watching his easy rapport with Megan and Cameron and Coralee only reinforced how stiff and uncomfortable he always seemed with her.

"Sorry to drop in like this without an appointment," he said, and she realized with a start he was talking to her. "I was wondering if there's any chance you could take a look at my arm? Something doesn't quite feel right about it."

He wanted *her* to look at his arm? This, from the man who had endured her ministrations the night before like she was shoving bamboo shoots under his fingernails?

He had just come from a morning spent at the University of Utah Medical Center. If his arm was bothering him so much, why didn't he just have someone there check it out?

"Of course," she managed through her shock. "I can do it now. We were just about to go to lunch."

"Do you want me to stick around?" Coralee asked.

"No, that's all right. I know you're meeting your sister for lunch at the diner. Go ahead."

Lauren led Daniel to an exam room. "Uh, do you want to unbutton your shirt?" She could feel her face flush at the question and prayed he didn't notice.

He leaned against the exam table and folded his arms across his chest—including the injured one in question. "No. I just used that as an excuse so I could talk to you without Coralee overhearing our conversation. I didn't realize she would be leaving anyway or I wouldn't have had to come up with a good story."

"Right. Coralee is harder to lie to than my mother."

"You lie to your mother, Dr. Maxwell? I'm shocked."

"I know. I'm a terrible person."

A muscle twitched in his cheek but he didn't give in to a full-fledged smile. "What did you tell Coralee about the bandage?" he asked.

"The truth. Or mostly the truth. I told her I had an accident at the hospital while checking on a patient."

"I think that's wise. I know she can be discreet, but the fewer people who know what's going on, the better."

"It wasn't really that. I just didn't want to worry her. Coralee is a bit of a mother hen, especially with my own mother living six hours away now."

She paused. "While you're here, you might as well let me take a look at your shoulder."

He looked less than enthralled at the idea. "That's really not necessary. I'm fine."

"Humor me. I want to make sure you're not starting with any infection. You can tell me what happened this morning at the hospital while I check you out. Your injury, I mean."

She wanted to bite her tongue for adding that last part so quickly, especially when he gave her a long, measuring look. She geared up for an argument about her demand, but either he was too tired to put up much of a fuss or his arm really *was* bothering him.

After a moment, his fingers went to the buttons of his uniform shirt and he started working them free. Lauren refused to acknowledge the ripple of her insides as he started baring all that smooth skin and hard muscles. He was a patient, for heaven's sake. She had to treat him with all the professionalism and courtesy she showed all her other patients.

She pulled the bandage away to find a little redness and swelling around the wound site.

He flinched when she touched it and she chewed her lip. If she needed a reminder to keep her mind away from him as a very attractive man, there it was. He obviously didn't like her touching him, even in a professional capacity.

She needed to remember that and forget about how her hands itched to smooth over him.

By the time she finally stepped away from him and shoved her hands into the pockets of her plum-colored sweater, Daniel was sweating and light-headed from holding his breath the whole time she had her hands on him.

He tried to hide his deep inhale behind a cough.

"Everything looks fine," she said. "A little red and swollen, but that's not out of the ordinary. If you notice any of that starting to spread at all, make sure you let me know."

Her voice was cool and brisk and he did his best to match it.

"I'll do that," he said. He fumbled with his buttons with fingers that felt big and awkward, as if they were bandaged, too.

He sure as hell hoped his arm healed soon because he couldn't endure her touching him again.

Okay, there was a lie he knew he couldn't sneak past either Lauren's mother or Coralee Jenkins. The bare-bones truth was just the opposite. He *did* want her hands on him, just not in any kind of medical setting.

"Now tell me how Rosa is doing?"

He cleared his throat, shifting gears back to what he knew he should be focusing on. "She was fine when I left an hour ago. Exhausted, since she didn't get much sleep before Cale and Gage McKinnon showed up and she had to go through it all again."

"Cale and his partner are handling the case?" Lauren asked. "That's a relief."

"Her imprisonment, rape and attempted murder definitely fall under their jurisdiction in the Crimes Against Children Unit," he answered. "We don't know if all the possible victims are under the legal age, but since Rosa will be the star witness and she's only fifteen, CAC will be spearheading the investigation."

"Great. With you or Cale both on the case, whoever did this will be behind bars in no time."

"I hope so, but I'm afraid it's not going to be that easy. The real reason I stopped by was to let you know she's been moved to a more secure location in the hospital. Even though you're the physician on record, you're going to need the access information before the guards will let you in. Assuming you're still planning to stop by, anyway."

"Of course."

He nodded, not at all surprised. Lauren was a dedicated doctor, completely committed to her patients. He would have been surprised if she *hadn't* been planning to drive to the city again that night.

"It's still not the ideal situation. I don't believe this Mata or the people he's working with will just give up trying to shut her mouth, but for now this is the best we can do, moving her to a more secure location and keeping security posted at her room at all times."

"I hope it's enough. What about when she's released?"

"We're still trying to work that out." He fought back a yawn. "The FBI is trying to find a good placement for her. She'll have to stick around to testify to the grand jury while the FBI gathers enough evidence to break up the smuggling and prostitution ring so they can make arrests. How much longer do you think Rosa will need to stay in the hospital?"

"Under normal circumstances, I would probably keep her at least a few more days, probably through the weekend. She hasn't had prenatal care throughout the pregnancy. That complicates things. I would recommend careful monitoring for the rest of her pregnancy, especially given the nature of the assault and the fact that she's already had some early contractions."

"I'll give the FBI a call and let them know they should plan on having a new placement for her by the day after tomorrow, at the latest."

"Will you let me know how things are going?" she asked.

"Of course."

He shrugged into his coat and was putting on his hat to leave when she touched his arm. "Daniel, how long since you slept last?"

As if her words finally pierced whatever force of will was keeping him functioning, he was suddenly so tired he wanted to lean his forehead against her and fall asleep right there.

"Yesterday morning, six a.m.," he admitted.

"You need some rest. I'm sure you don't need me to tell you that. You've been an athlete and you know it's not at all healthy for you to burn yourself out like this."

He hadn't had anyone fuss over him for a long time. He wasn't quite sure how to handle

it. "There have been a few unusual circumstances the last twenty-four hours keeping me
awake. But I'm heading home now. I have
high hopes I'll be able to fall into my big,
warm bed and not wake up again until my
shift tonight."

She still look worried but she managed a smile.
"Do that. We need you strong and healthy."

He wasn't at all sure why color rose on her
delicate cheekbones, but he found it fascinating.

"The town, I mean," she said quickly. "If you
wear yourself out, you're bound to compromise
your immune system and leave yourself open to
all kinds of infections."

"Right. We wouldn't want that, would we?
Don't worry about me. You've got enough on
your plate taking care of the whole town. I'll
be fine."

Did she have any kind of drugs he could take
that would give him a stronger immune system
when it came to her? he wondered as he finally
left her clinic and drove toward home. Some-

thing that would keep her from invading his thoughts and completely taking over?

He had told her these last twenty-four hours had been full of unusual circumstances. Right at the top of that list was the fact that he had spent more time in her company since he walked into her clinic yesterday evening than he ever had. Even when he hadn't been with her physically, she hadn't been far from his mind.

Was it wishful thinking on his part to think perhaps she wasn't completely immune to him, either? He had sensed several times last night and again this morning that she might be softening toward him. Things between them seemed easier, somehow. Slightly more comfortable.

He liked it. More than liked it.

He drove past her massive childhood home, the biggest house in town, all wrought iron and elegant cornices and perfectly groomed grounds. She had sold the place after her father's death to a young couple from Utah County. Nice people. The husband commuted to Orem every day to work in the state's own version of Silicon Valley and the wife volunteered in the little Moose Springs library.

A few blocks later, he reached his own house, the same four-room clapboard house where his parents had raised their family. He had fixed it up before his mom lost her fight with cancer, added a family room off the back and another bathroom, but it was still a small house on a tiny lot.

Daniel sighed. Here was the hard reminder he needed. Lauren had been raised in luxury and comfort, the pampered only child of two doting parents. He had grown up fighting for one minuscule bathroom with two brothers and a sister.

The biggest obstacle between them wasn't really his humble upbringing or her socially elevated one. He might see that as a glaring difference, but he had a feeling Lauren really wouldn't care about that.

She *would,* however, care about his role in her father's downfall and subsequent suicide.

No amount of wishing on his part could change that.

Chapter 6

She was ready for a vacation.

Friday morning dawned stormy and cold as she drove the busy canyon from Moose Springs to the hospital in Salt Lake City. Her wipers worked steadily but they couldn't keep the big, juicy flakes off the window and she was grateful for the all-wheel-drive of her car.

Lauren had grown up driving in snow but she still wasn't crazy about it. She always found it stressful and demanding. Winter driving wasn't so bad in tiny Moose Springs, where she never encountered more than a few other cars on the road, but the early-morning commute into the city was another story altogether.

By the time she pulled her Volvo into the parking lot at the hospital, her shoulders were tight and her fingers ached from gripping the steering wheel. She climbed out of her vehicle and stepped into four inches of snow that hadn't been scraped off the parking lot yet.

Maybe later in the week when things were settled with Rosa, she ought to give in to her mother's pressure tactics and head to southern Utah for a few days. Soaking up the sun in St. George seemed like a lovely idea right about now.

A week of leisure time would be a decadent luxury. She hadn't had a break longer than a quick weekend in five years and the grim truth was, she wouldn't be taking this one if not for Coralee and her anniversary cruise.

A little respite would be good for her, a chance to recharge and remember why she started in medicine in the first place. And some sunshine right about now might lift her spirits out of this funk.

She walked through the door, stomping snow off her boots. The first person she saw in the lobby was Kendall Fox, talking to a couple of women in scrubs. He looked ruggedly handsome, with that sun-streaked blond hair and skier's tan, and she had to admit her ego enjoyed a nice little boost when his eyes lit up with pleasure at the sight of her.

He excused himself from the other nurses and headed toward her. "Lauren! I was hoping I would bump into you today."

"Oh?" Why couldn't she summon a little attraction for vivid blue eyes and a man who knew just what to do with them? Instead, all she could think about were Daniel's eyes, dark and warm and solemn.

"Yeah. Don't ask me how I did it but I scored an invite for one of the huge after-screening parties up at Deer Valley tonight. I need to find a gorgeous woman to escort, and of course I thought of you. What time can I pick you up?"

She had to admit to a flicker of temptation. When he wasn't hitting on anything that moved, Kendall could be funny and charming and attentive. She was tired of living like a nun. Was it wrong to want a little diversion from the solitude of her life?

A moment's reflection was all she needed to reinforce what a lousy idea that would be. She wasn't at all interested in a player like Kendall, who probably had the cell phone numbers of every available female at the hospital and a few unavailable ones as well.

If she went out with him and had to spend the evening fighting off his inevitable moves, she would be left more depressed than ever.

"Sorry. I've got plans tonight," she lied.

"Break them. Come on. How often do you get to mix with the Hollywood glitterati in your little Podunk Cow Springs?"

"*Moose* Springs. You're right, almost never.

And yet somehow I still manage to lead a rewarding, fulfilling life."

"You want fulfillment, I can provide it beyond your wildest dreams," he murmured in her ear.

She barely restrained from rolling her eyes. Okay, forget lousy idea. Going out with Kendall Fox, even for the sake of a little conversation, would be a nightmare of epic proportions. She would spend the whole night fighting off his wandering hands and wishing she were somewhere else. Or at least that *he* was *someone* else.

She started to answer—or at least tell him to back off and give her a little room to breathe here—but the words died in her throat. Some instinct had her looking up and she was horrified to find Daniel standing ten feet away from them, watching her out of those dark eyes of his that suddenly didn't look remotely warm.

"Daniel!" she exclaimed. She had no reason to feel so absurdly guilty but that didn't keep hot water from washing over her cheekbones.

She quickly stepped away from Kendall.

"Lauren. Dr. Fox." She couldn't tell if that reserve in his voice was politeness or disdain.

She forced a cheerful smile. On the one hand, she was grateful to have a ready excuse to escape Kendall's persistence. On the other, she would have preferred anyone other than Daniel be the one to ride to her social rescue.

"I imagine we're here to see the same person," she said brightly. "I'll walk up with you."

An instant of surprise registered in his eyes, but he quickly veiled it. "All right."

Kendall's features tightened with annoyance. He opened his mouth but she cut him off. The last thing she needed right now was for Daniel to be standing nearby when she told Kendall she wasn't interested in ever going out with him.

"Have a good time at your party," she said, hoping her refusal was firm and clear, then led the way through the hospital lobby toward the bank of elevators.

She and Daniel were the only two people

taking the elevator. In such close quarters she was acutely aware of his size and how small and fragile she always felt next to him.

He look rested, she thought. Or at least not quite as exhausted as he had two days earlier in her office, when she had seen him last.

"We need to talk," he said abruptly, when the doors glided closed. He smelled of soap and clean male and he was freshly shaved. It was all she could do not to run her hand along that strong, hard jawline.

She blinked. "Okay."

"Are you planning to write discharge orders today?"

Right. Rosa's case. What else would they have to talk about? "I can't know that yet until I have a chance to look at the chart and see how her pain level was during the night and whether she's had any repeat contractions. If she had a quiet night, I don't really have any reason to keep her longer. Unless you think she's safer in the hospital."

"I don't," he said as the elevator lurched to a stop on Rosa's floor. The doors opened and Lauren was vastly relieved to step out into the hall, where she could breathe without inhaling his delicious scent.

"I got a call from hospital security this morning that there was a suspicious man lurking around here last night just as visiting hours were closing," he went on. "He walked down the hall, saw the security guard outside Rosa's room, then backtracked. They tried to detain him for questioning but he disappeared. I have to believe they'll try again."

Her hands tightened on her laptop case. "Does Rosa know?"

"Not unless security or the FBI told her. Cale is meeting me here this morning to talk about a safe house situation for her."

"It's good of them to keep you in the loop."

"I'm making sure they do on this one. She trusted me enough to tell me what was happening and I won't betray that trust by just turning her over to the FBI without making sure they have a good placement for her."

When they reached the secured unit, they found Cale and his partner Gage McKinnon standing at the nurse's station. Lauren had met Gage the summer before during the search for Cameron Vance. She smiled a greeting and asked after his wife, Allie, and his daughters and infant son, whom she had met at Megan and Cale's wedding.

They exchanged small talk for a moment, then Lauren excused herself. "I need to check in on my patient," she said.

Rosa was sitting up eating breakfast and watching Spanish soap operas when she walked in. The girl smiled at her. Three days after her attack, the bruises and swelling were beginning to fade and Lauren could see the fragile loveliness begin to emerge.

She greeted the girl in her painfully precise Spanish and asked how she was feeling.

"Good. Better," Rosa said with a shy smile.

"I see that. You're looking good," Lauren said. "Did you sleep well?"

Rosa shrugged and said something quickly in Spanish that she didn't quite catch.

"Sorry. Slower, please," Lauren begged.

Rosa repeated her statement and this time Lauren caught the key word. *Nightmare.*

"I'm sorry," she said softly. "Those will fade in time, I promise."

This, she knew from experience. Her own had faded some time ago, though once in a while they still reared their ugly head. Two nights before— the night after she had caught the man in Rosa's hospital room smothering the life out of her and he had struck her—Lauren's own nightmare had returned for the first time in a long time.

In her dream she had been eighteen again, trapped and helpless and frightened.

This time she had fought back, as she hadn't dared do then, and had kicked and clawed and finally stabbed her attacker with a conveniently placed scalpel.

If she had the right words in Spanish, she would have told Rosa that nightmares could sometimes be empowering, could sometimes alert a woman to the amazing truth that she had grown past her fears into a capable, strong woman.

She didn't have that kind of command of the language, though, so she only squeezed her shoulder. "It will get better," she promised again.

She finished her exam of the girl and then returned to the hallway, where Daniel stood talking to the FBI agents.

"What's the verdict?" Cale asked. "Do you think she's in any condition to be released?"

Daniel wasn't the only one who felt protective toward the girl. She folded her arms across her chest. "Before I'm prepared to answer that, I need to know if you have a safe place for her to go."

"You sound just like Dan. I'll give you the same answer I gave him. Not yet, I'm afraid. At least not any option I'm all that crazy about. Our best possibility is a safe house we use down in the Avenues, close enough that we can get her to the hospital in just a few minutes if we need to."

"Sounds perfect," Daniel said.

"Only trouble is, it's not available right now and it won't be for another few days," McKinnon said.

"What's behind Door Number Two?" Lauren asked.

"You won't like it," Cale predicted.

"Try me."

"We thought maybe we could check her into a hotel near the hospital until she testifies to the grand jury next week."

Lauren narrowed her eyes. "No way. You can't possibly be considering dumping a frightened, pregnant girl who doesn't speak English into a cold, impersonal hotel somewhere."

"I know that. That's the dilemma we're facing. We have agents and safe houses in other states where we could send her, but we need Rosa close for her grand jury testimony. Are you sure she's ready to be discharged?"

She wanted to tell him no, that Rosa should stay right where she was, but she couldn't lie in good conscience, not when the bed should be used for someone who really needed it.

"There's no medical reason for her to stay," she admitted. "Her condition is stable and she is recovering nicely from her injuries. But I'm telling you right now that if you plan to abandon this girl in some seedy motel somewhere, I will damn well make something up to keep her here!"

Daniel had to smile as Lauren's impassioned words rang through the hallway, drawing the attention of several nurses at the desk. He knew she was a good doctor, but this was the first time he realized how committed she was to the welfare of her patients.

No, he didn't want to cheer. He wanted to pull her into his arms and kiss her until they were both breathless.

"Do you have any other suggestions?" McKinnon asked.

"Yes," Lauren said firmly. "She can stay with me."

"What?!" Daniel and both of the FBI agents exclaimed the word at the same time.

"I'll take her to my place in Moose Springs until your safe house is ready. After today, I'm off for a week and I can stay with her and watch over her, keep her company, monitor her for more contractions. I can give her one-on-one attention."

"Absolutely not," Daniel snapped.

Lauren lifted her chin, apparently not at all intimidated by three menacing males. "Why not? It's a perfect solution. She'll be absolutely safe at my house. Who would ever think to look for her there? And I can care for her far better than any FBI agent stuck in a safe house with her!"

"It's completely out of the question. Isn't that right?" he demanded of the FBI agents.

He was stunned when he glanced at Cale and found his lips pursed as if he were giving the idea serious consideration. "I don't know. It's certainly an option."

"It is *not* an option." He wanted to shake Lauren and Cale both. And maybe McKinnon for good measure, even though the other FBI agent hadn't said a word. "How can you even consider putting a civilian in that kind of danger?"

"What danger?" Cale asked. "It makes a lot of sense. Rosa needs a safe place where her medical condition can be closely monitored. This seems like a good solution and if we handle this right, the smuggling ring would have no way to connect Rosa with Lauren."

"Other than the minor little fact that Lauren is her *doctor,* for hell's sake!"

He was apparently talking to himself. Lauren ignored his objections—and so did the FBI agents, whom he had always considered reasonable men before this.

"We would need to figure out a way to sneak her out of the hospital in case they're watching the entrances and exits," McKinnon said. "Your address isn't in public record, is it?"

"No," Lauren said. "I use a PO Box for all my

personal correspondence and everything else comes to the clinic."

"This could work," Cale said. "We'll have to run it past the brass to get their input but I think this could definitely work as a temporary option for only a few days until our safe house is available and our staffing issues resolve a little. What do you think, Gage?"

"It can't hurt that your house is just a mile away from Dr. Maxwell's, for additional support if it's needed."

"True."

Before he could say anything else, a cell phone rang suddenly. The two agents exchanged looks and McKinnon answered his phone in a low voice. A moment later, he hung up.

"Sorry, we've got to run," he said, heading toward the door. "We just got a break in another case we're working."

"What about Rosa?" Daniel asked. "We need to settle this!"

"We'll make a few phone calls and see if we can put the wheels in motion," Cale said. "We'll get back to you later today."

To his intense frustration, they both hurried toward the elevator before Daniel could raise the whole host of objections crowding through his mind. He and Lauren were left standing alone.

"You don't have to stand there glaring at me like I just ran over your foot or something," Lauren said. "I think it's a good idea."

"I think you're insane. And I think Davis and McKinnon are right there with you in Crazy Town."

"I didn't see *you* coming up with anything else! You know they can't just toss her into a hotel somewhere. She's been raped and abused and nearly strangled. She's frightened and alone and she needs friends more than anything else. Right now, we're the only people she knows and trusts in the entire country!"

"What if they figure out where she is somehow and follow you to Moose Springs?"

"They won't."

"What if they do?" he pressed, his attention on the stark white bandage on her cheek. "You've already been hurt once watching out for her. You have no idea what kind of resources these people might have. They found her here, didn't they? I sure as hell don't need that kind of trouble in my town."

He could see the temperature in her eyes drop well below freezing. "Since when is Moose Springs *your* town? I don't believe I need your permission to invite a guest to my home."

"In this case, you do," he snapped. "Despite their misguided enthusiasm for the idea, Cale and Gage and the others at the FBI will never agree unless I give the final okay. I'm the local law, I get the last word. That's the way it works. I can make all kinds of trouble for them until they decide maybe it's not such a great plan after all."

"You would do that? Put up a fuss, just so you can keep your town clear of the riffraff?"

He didn't think he had ever seen her so angry. Hurt, yes. Devastated, definitely. When he and the chief of police had showed up at her big, ornate childhood home to tell her and her mother about R.J.'s suicide in jail, she had been desolate with grief.

Now, she was just pissed. He couldn't quite understand it.

"Why is this so important to you?" he asked. "You've treated other crime victims, plenty of them. I've brought more than my share to your clinic myself. You always treat them with compassion and professionalism, but not to the point where you want to take them home with you. Why are you so invested in Rosa's situation?"

He thought he saw something flicker in her eyes, something murky and dark, but she quickly veiled it.

"She's my patient," Lauren said briskly. "Beyond that, Rosa is a courageous young girl who has survived a terrible ordeal. I want to help her. Right now, this seems like the best way I can do that. With the clinic closing next week, I have plenty of time to spend with her. It works out all the way around."

Daniel knew Lauren was devoted to her patients, the kind of rare doctor who was available in case of emergencies 24/7.

This was the perfect example of her dedication, that she wanted to go so far, possibly put herself in harm's way for the second time in a week, to help a young girl she had only met a few days earlier.

"You should be taking a vacation, not baby-sitting a patient. What were you planning to do before this came up?"

Lauren shrugged. "I thought about following the sun and going to southern Utah for a few days to visit my mother," she admitted. "But I can do that anytime, really. Over a long weekend, even. I couldn't go right now and have a good time, knowing that I left Rosa huddled in some cold, impersonal hotel room with strangers who probably don't care what she's been through or how much strength it took for her to come forward and report what happened to her."

She tempered her tone. "You're the one who said you wouldn't turn her over to the FBI unless they had a good placement for her. They don't and so I'm coming up with my own."

In a twisted kind of way, the idea *did* make sense. Moose Springs was completely off the beaten track, a quiet little town no one would ever suspect as the safe haven for a key federal witness in a human smuggling case.

He had to admit, Rosa would probably do better if she spent her first few days out of the hospital with someone who could watch her carefully for any signs she might be overdoing things—and she would definitely do better with people who cared about her than distant FBI agents more concerned about their case than a young girl's bruised psyche.

He sighed heavily, already regretting what he was about to do.

"All right. If you want to go ahead with this crazy idea. I won't stand in your way. On one condition."

"What condition?" she asked, her voice wary.

"I'm part of the deal."

She stared at him, shock widening her eyes. "You what?"

"You can call it chauvinism, you can call it machismo, you can call it whatever the hell you want. But I'm not letting the two of you stay out at your place alone when Rosa has already twice been targeted for murder and you've been injured. You want to take her home with you, fine. But I'm coming, too."

Chapter 7

Several hours later, Lauren stood just inside her storm door, watching in the light cast from her porch light as Daniel helped Rosa out of the backseat of a nondescript sedan she didn't recognize.

It wasn't his, she knew. On his personal time, Daniel drove a big white pickup truck that only served to make him seem more darkly gorgeous behind the wheel.

Maybe it belonged to the sheriff's department. Or perhaps the FBI had provided transportation, since they weren't able to provide much else in the way of support.

What had she done? Daniel Galvez was coming to stay at her house for at least a day or two, possibly longer. He would eat at her table, he would use her shower, he would fill every corner of her little house with that huge presence.

She hadn't really planned out her impulsive offer for Rosa to stay at her house back at the hospital this morning. The words had escaped her mouth before she had fully considered the ramifications.

If she had taken the time to think it through, she might have anticipated that Daniel would insist on stepping forward to provide protection for Rosa—and for *her*.

If the thought had even crossed her mind, she probably would have rescinded her suggestion and consigned poor Rosa to a hotel.

No, she thought as she watched them make their careful way up the walk she had just finished shoveling. She still would have demanded Rosa stay here. She just would have been better prepared to tell Daniel all the reasons his presence was not required—not required and certainly not at all good for her sense of self-preservation.

She watched him lift Rosa over a rough section of sidewalk, the solid bulk of his shoulders not even flexing at the effort, and her insides ached.

She held the door open for them, giving Rosa a wide, welcoming smile. She did her best to keep that welcome on her features when she faced Daniel, but she guessed some of her reservations must have filtered through when his mouth tightened and his dark eyes grew cool.

"Come in," she said in Spanish. "I'm so pleased you are here." Lauren tried to include both of them in that statement, even though that self-protective part of her nature wanted to shove Daniel back onto the porch and lock the door behind him.

"*Gracias,*" Rosa said quietly. She looked tired, Lauren thought with concern.

"Come. Sit," she urged, and led them both to the open living area off the kitchen. In the rare hours she was home, this was the space she tended to utilize the most.

A fire crackled in the fireplace and the room was several degrees warmer than the rest of the house. She settled Rosa in her own favorite chair by the fire and tucked a blanket around her.

"How was your drive?" she asked Daniel.

"Long. We traded vehicles three times in case anybody followed us and we took the most complicated route possible."

"Did you see anyone?"

"I never saw a tail, except Gage and Cale. They followed us to Park City and then turned around. I don't think anyone saw us leave. We borrowed an ambulance for the first leg of the journey and sneaked her out in that."

Worry creased his features. "Just because we made it here safely doesn't mean we're out of the woods yet, though. This whole situation makes me itchy."

"I know." The gravity of his expression gave her pause. She prayed she wasn't putting Daniel in harm's way. She couldn't back out of this now, no matter how much she dreaded several days of enforced intimacy with him.

She turned her attention to her patient. "Rosa, how are you feeling?" she asked in Spanish.

The girl tried to smile, but Lauren could see the circles under her eyes and the strained exhaustion tugging down the corners of her mouth. She murmured something in a low voice that Lauren didn't quite catch and pointed to her head, but the doctor in her didn't need the words to know what her patient was communicating.

"Your head hurts? I can give you something for it, something safe for the baby. I've made some dinner for you, but I think you should rest first until you feel better."

"*Sí.*" Relief flickered in her dark eyes. "*Gracias.*"

Lauren helped her from the chair and showed

her to the small guest room she kept ready for her mother's visits.

Since Janine had plenty of reason to hate coming back to Moose Springs and usually avoided the place as if everyone in it had a highly contagious form of leprosy, the room had rarely been used. As a result, it was rather sparsely decorated, just a bed with a pale lavender floral bedspread, a plain dresser and a bedside table.

Rosa gazed around wide-eyed, as if she were walking into the posh suite of a four-star hotel. Tears formed in her eyes and she whispered her thanks in Spanish several times.

Lauren's heart twisted for what this poor girl had endured. Impulsively, she hugged her. "I'm happy you're here," she murmured again in Spanish. "Rest. I will bring you something for your headache. The soup will wait until you're feeling better."

With a relieved sigh, Rosa nodded and sat on the edge of the bed. Knowing it would be a difficult task with the cast on her arm and the pain of her cracked ribs, Lauren knelt and helped her out of her shoes. She wore shiny white tennis shoes with pink stripes and Lauren wondered where they had come from.

All her clothes—even her parka—looked new and Lauren was embarrassed she hadn't thought about what Rosa would wear from the hospital since the girl's own ragged clothes had been ripped and bloody after the attack.

She wondered if the FBI agents had the foresight to provide them, but some instinct told her exactly who had been thoughtful enough to remember such an important detail.

Daniel.

Her stomach gave a funny little flip when she pictured him in a shoe department somewhere picking out white tennis shoes with pink stripes on the sides.

Pushing away her silly reaction, she settled Rosa into bed, drawing the fluffy comforter around her, then went in search of her medicine.

When she returned from giving it to Rosa, she found Daniel in the entryway stamping snow off his boots and carrying a large dark duffel in one hand and a small blue suitcase in the other.

"This is the rest of Rosa's stuff." He handed over the suitcase.

"Did you buy it for her?" she asked, though she already knew the answer.

He shrugged. "There's not much in there but I tried to think of everything she might need. Toothbrush, a nightgown, socks, that kind of thing. One of the nurses helped me guess the sizes."

She imagined the nurses would help him with anything he might ask when he looked at them out of those sexy dark eyes that seemed to see inside a woman's deepest desires…

"Where do you want me to stow my gear?" he said.

"Oh. Right." Flustered, she drew herself back to the conversation. "I have a small room I use as an office, right next to Rosa's. It has a couch that folds out. It's not the most comfortable bed in the world but I'm not really set up for a lot of houseguests. I'm afraid I don't have anything else."

Except for my bed.

The thought whispered through her mind with an insidious appeal she found both horrifying and seductive.

She was in serious trouble here if she couldn't go ten seconds without entertaining completely inappropriate thoughts about the man.

"I'm sure I've slept in worse places," he answered. "It will be fine, don't worry."

Easy for *him* to say. He wasn't the one who couldn't seem to focus on anything else but the way his broad shoulders filled her small entry, how his size and strength seemed to dwarf all the perfectly normal-sized furnishings in her house.

"You'll have to point the way."

She blinked. "The way?"

"To the foldout couch."

"Oh, yes. Of course. The office is the second

door on the right. The first one is Rosa's room. Mine is across the hall and there's a guest bathroom next to that. I'll show you."

She led the way down the short hallway and opened her office door. He set his bag inside and she showed him the bathroom across the hall.

"It's a little small," she apologized, wondering if he would even fit in the shower.

As soon as the thought entered her mind, she shoved it away quickly. She did *not* need to go there.

"I'm sure it will be fine."

"There's room in the medicine cabinet for anything you need to put there. Razors, your toothbrush, whatever."

For some ridiculous reason, her face heated at that. It seemed terribly intimate to have a man here. How pathetic must her love life be if she could blush at having a man in her bathroom?

"Thanks," he murmured, and she had the oddest feeling he didn't find this whole situation any easier to handle.

"I, uh, fixed some soup earlier if you're hungry," she said after a moment. "It's all ready. Chicken and black bean."

"Sounds great. Thanks."

They returned to the kitchen and Lauren quickly went to the stove to stir the soup, then reached into the cupboard for a bowl.

"There is silverware already on the table. Just sit wherever you would like and I'll dish it for you."

He stood in the doorway. "You don't have to wait on me, Lauren. That wasn't part of the deal."

"You're a guest in my home," she said. "You might be an uninvited one, but you're still a guest."

He laughed a little abruptly at her tartness. "I guess that's plain enough."

"Sit down, Daniel. You can have some soup, even if you are on guard-dog duty."

A muscle twitched in his cheek. "Well, if you want the truth, I haven't had time to eat all day and whatever you're cooking smells delicious."

"I'm not much of a cook," she confessed, "but I do have a few good soup recipes."

He finally complied, though he didn't look happy about it, and she filled two bowls with the steaming soup, flavored with cilantro, lime and jalapeño peppers.

"Here you go," she said, setting both bowls on the plates she had already set earlier. She gestured to the garnishes already on the table— shredded cheese, tortilla strips, sour cream, more jalapeños and cilantro. "You can put whatever garnishes you want in it. It's kind of a flavor-your-own deal."

"It looks great. I'm sorry you went to so much trouble."

"It wasn't any trouble."

It did look delicious, she had to admit. Just the thing for a snowy Friday night. She put a little grated cheddar in hers and a few baked tortilla strips, but she wasn't at all surprised when he piled on the jalapeños.

He seemed so close here at her small square

table, huge and overpowering. She was acutely aware of the broadness of his shoulders and the blunt strength in his arms and the scent of him, leathery and male.

So much for enjoying the soup. She couldn't taste anything, she was far too twitchy just being this close to him.

This certainly wasn't the first meal they had ever shared. Moose Springs was a small town with very little in the way of entertainment except the annual Fourth of July breakfast and the August Moosemania celebration. Everybody turned out for those, and over the years she and Daniel had almost certainly shared a table.

They had many of the same friends in common—Mason and Jane Keller, Cale and Megan Davis. But even those times they had attended the same dinner parties or barbecues, there had always been others around to provide a buffer.

She couldn't remember ever sharing a meal with him alone like this. For some reason, it had all the awkwardness of a blind date—something she made it a practice to avoid at all costs.

"I was wrong," he said after a moment. "Your soup isn't delicious. It's divine."

She mustered a smile. "Thank you."

"This is the perfect thing to warm the blood on a cold winter night," he said, then winced at the inanity of his conversation. Not only was it a banal thing to say, it was patently untrue.

His blood didn't need any more temperature spikes. He only had to sit within a few feet of Lauren to be plenty warm. Before the evening was done, he was very much afraid he would be sweltering.

He was doing his best to focus on the meal in front of him and not on Lauren, with her soft blond hair pulled back in a loose ponytail and her slim feet in fuzzy socks and her skin rosy and flushed in the warm kitchen.

It was an impossible task. Even with the bandage on her cheek, she was so lovely here in her house, sexy and soft, and with every taste of soup she took, he wanted to whip the spoon out of her mouth, throw it against the wall and devour those lips.

His body ached just breathing the same air. How ridiculous was that? He had always known he had a thing for her, but these last few days had just demonstrated it was far more than a little unrequited crush.

He was powerfully attracted to her. He couldn't remember ever reacting this way to a woman, this wild heat in his gut. Every nerve cell in his body seemed to quiver when she was anywhere around and he couldn't seem to focus on a thing but her.

She sipped her water, and when she returned the water goblet to the table, a tiny drop clung to her bottom lip. He couldn't seem to stop staring at it, wondering what she would do if he reached across the table and licked it off.

"What do you usually eat?" she asked.

He blinked away the unbidden fantasy, harshly

reminding himself he was here to do a job, to protect Lauren and her houseguest, not to indulge himself by wishing for the impossible.

He forgot what she had asked. "Sorry?" he managed.

"We keep the same kind of hours and I know you don't have much more time than I do. I just wondered if you eat every meal on the run or if you take time to cook a decent meal once in a while."

"I'm not a great cook but I do try to fix a few things on my days off. Whenever I can, I cook extra so I have things to warm up during the week. I think my deputies and Peggy and the other dispatchers think I live on nothing but cold cereal and frozen dinners. They must feel sorry for me, because it seems like somebody is always inviting me over for dinner."

"Like the department stray dog?"

He smiled. "Something like that."

She returned his smile. Daniel stared at the way it lightened her features, made her look not much older than Rosa. His breath seemed to catch in his throat and he did his best to remind himself of all the reasons he couldn't kiss that soft mouth.

"While Rosa and I are here, I really don't expect you to wait on me. I'll do my share of the cooking. Why don't I take breakfast?"

"Since cold cereal is your specialty?" she teased.

"I can fix more than cold cereal," he protested. "For your information, Miss Doubter, I'm great at toast and can usually manage to boil water for oatmeal, too, without burning the house down."

"I hope so. I'm fairly fond of my house," she said.

The conversation reminded him of something he meant to bring up with her earlier. "If the FBI doesn't make the offer, my department will pick up the tab for the groceries Rosa and I use while we're here. Just keep a tally and send the bill to my office when this is over."

Her spoon froze halfway to her mouth, then she returned it to her soup bowl with a clatter. "Absolutely not!" she exclaimed.

He wasn't quite prepared for her vehemence. "Why not? Rosa is ultimately my responsibility. You're not obligated to pay for her room and board, my office should be taking care of that."

"Forget it, Daniel. I'm the one who insisted she stay here. She is a guest in my house and I will take care of feeding her."

"You didn't want me as part of the package."

"No. I didn't," she snapped, and though he knew it was crazy, he couldn't help feeling a little hurt. How could he burn for her so hotly when she didn't even want him around?

"Fine, we'll compromise," he said. "You can pay for Rosa's food and I'll pay my own."

"This is stupid. I've already bought enough groceries to last a week or more for all three of us. Just take your share out of the huge collective mental ledger everyone seems to be keeping, the one marked 'Maxwell family debt' and clearly labeled 'unpaid.'"

She clamped her teeth together as soon as the bitter words were out and looked as if she regretted saying anything.

Is that what she thought? That everyone believed she owed her heart and soul to Moose Springs, just because her father was a crook?

"There is no collective ledger, huge or otherwise."

"Right." She rose, her usually fluid movements suddenly jerky and abrupt as she started clearing away the dishes. He had been considering asking for a second helping, but he forgot all about it now, struck that she could entertain such a misguided notion.

"Everyone knows you're not responsible for what your father did, Lauren."

"Do they?"

He frowned at her pointed question. Okay, he had to admit there might be some validity in her bitterness. The other day with Dale Richins, he had experienced just a taste of what she might encounter in certain circles. The scorn, the disdain.

It suddenly bugged the hell out of him that anybody could blame an innocent girl for her father's crimes.

"In their hearts, everyone knows that. But some people in town are just more stubborn and pigheaded on this issue than they ought to be. How can it be your fault? You were only a girl when he first, uh…"

His voice trailed off and he wasn't quite sure how to couch his words in polite terms.

"Go ahead and finish it, Daniel. When R.J. first starting dipping his fingers into the city's meager financial well."

"Right. You were just a child. Anybody who can blame you for what R.J. did is being mean and stupid."

"Intellectually, I know that. It doesn't make the digs and slurs in the grocery store any easier to deal with it. My father paid for my medical school tuition out of stolen money—which means, in effect, that the people of this town paid for my education. Do you think I'm not aware of that every time I look at my diploma?"

He had no idea she tied the two things together, her father's embezzlement and her own medical school bills. Guilt spasmed through him at his own role in this whole thing. If she knew the truth, she probably would have added rat poison to the soup.

"Lauren—"

"This town owns me, body and soul. My father made sure of that. I can never leave here, no matter all the slights and slurs and whispers I have to endure. They paid for my education and I am obligated to damn well give them their money's worth."

She shoved a dish in the dishwasher with a clatter. "But you know, it doesn't matter what I do, how much I give. I can pour out my soul here in my practice, work twenty hours a day, treat anybody who walks through the door whether they have any intention of paying me or not. But I'll still always be crooked R. J. Maxwell's daughter."

"You can't change where you came from, Lauren, no matter how hard you try."

He should know. He had spent way too much time during his teenage years wishing he could belong to any other family in town except the dirt-poor Galvez family, with a mother who scrubbed toilets and a father who did every miserable grunt job that came along at R. J. Maxwell's construction company, for usually half as much as anybody else on the crew, just because he didn't have a green card.

Now, it shamed him deeply that he had ever considered his family inferior to anyone else.

He used to ride his bike past Lauren's grand house on Center Street and want everything inside there—furniture that matched and didn't come from Goodwill, a soft, pretty mother who smelled like flowers instead of disinfectant, his own bedroom instead of the crowded, chronically messy one he had to share with two annoying younger brothers.

He used to think Lauren's life was perfect. She had everything—money, brains, beauty. He wanted the kingdom, and in his deepest heart, he had wanted the beautiful golden princess who came along with it.

Over the years, he had learned that the kingdom was built on sand, the king was a fraud and a cheat, and the castle had been sold long ago to pay his bills.

But the princess.

Oh, yeah, he still wanted the princess.

"I know I can't change what my father did," she said quietly. "I live with it every day."

"You've done more to make things right than anyone could ever expect of you, Lauren. Anyone who doesn't see that, who doesn't admire and respect the hell out of you for what you've done here, is someone who doesn't deserve even a moment of your time."

At his words, something about her seemed to

crumble. One moment she was looking at him with defiance and bitterness and the next, her soft mouth trembled and she stared at him out of luminous blue eyes welling with tears.

"Ah, hell. I'm sorry. Don't cry, Lauren. Please don't cry."

He rose and pulled her into his arms. He couldn't help himself.

She sagged against his chest and her arms slid around him. To his vast and eternal relief, she sniffled a few times but she didn't let the tears loose. He held her close, burying his face in hair that smelled of jasmine and vanilla. After a moment, she stirred and lifted her face to his.

"I'm sorry. I try not to indulge in pity parties more than once or twice a month. You just caught me on a bad day."

"Don't mention it," he murmured, and then he couldn't help himself. He took what he had been fantasizing about since he walked into her house earlier.

Chapter 8

Her mouth was soft, delicious, like sinking into the best dream he had ever had. After one raw instant, his body revved into overdrive and he could focus on nothing but how incredibly right she felt in his arms.

He wanted to devour her, right there in her kitchen, just wrap his arms around her, drag her to the floor and consume every inch of her. Even as the wild need raged through him, ravaging his control, he forced himself to take things slow and easy, to hide his wild hunger behind a facade of soft, steady calm.

He hadn't been with a woman in a long time, but he knew that wasn't the reason why his vision dimmed and he suddenly couldn't seem to keep hold of a coherent thought.

That reason was simple, really. Lauren.

He couldn't quite believe she was here in his arms, the girl who had been affecting him in a strange, baffling way since he was a kid.

Even when he had been sixteen and big for his age, the toughest kid in school, he had dreamed of sweet Lauren Maxwell. The mayor's little girl, with her shiny blond ponytail and her soft, pretty hands and her wide, generous smile.

It had mortified him, this fascination with her, and even then he had known anything between them was an impossibility.

The taste of her seemed to soak through his bones and he couldn't seem to get enough. This was stupid, he knew. Monumentally stupid. Playing chicken with an express train kind of stupid.

He had to reign in his hunger. If he didn't, if he gave in to it, how could he ever return to the stiff politeness that had marked their relationship since her father's death?

He drew in a ragged breath and did his best to clamp down on the wild need raging through him.

He might have even succeeded if he hadn't heard the soft, seductive sound of his name on her lips, against his mouth, and felt her hands tremble over the muscles of his chest.

They had come this far. One more kiss wouldn't hurt anything. That's what he told himself, anyway.

And a tiny portion of his mind even believed it.

She was sliding into an endless canyon of sensation, surrounded by the heat and strength and leashed power of Daniel Galvez.

Somehow, she wouldn't have expected his

kiss to be so slow, so easy and gentle. Though she couldn't say she spent a great deal of time fantasizing about men and their kissing styles, if she had to guess Daniel's, she would have expected him to kiss a woman like the athlete he had been, fast and fierce and passionate.

Instead, he seduced her with softness, teasing and tasting and exploring. He nibbled her lips, he traced light designs on the bare skin of her neck with his fingertips, he rubbed his cheek against hers—and she found that light rasp of evening stubble against her skin far more evocative and sensual than a full-body massage.

He kissed her until every nerve ending inside her seemed to quiver, until she wanted to melt into him, to wrap her arms around his strong neck, press her body against his muscles and lose herself in him.

When she was young, she used to love it when Moose Springs held its annual celebration and the town paid for a small carnival for the children with giant inflatable slides and a

Tilt-o-Whirl and enough cotton candy to power the midway lights on juiced-up kid power alone.

Her favorite was the pony ride. Once, when she was probably seven or eight, her father had slipped the carnival workers a few extra dollars to let her just keep riding that little horse around and around. She probably rode for half an hour and she had never forgotten the magic of that night, with the lights flashing and the screams of children braving the more terrifying rides and the smell of popcorn and spun sugar and spilled sodas.

This was far more exhilarating than any long-ago pony ride. She didn't want the kiss to end, she just wanted to lock the cold, snowy world outside her kitchen and stay right here in his arms forever with this wild heat churning through her insides and this fragile tenderness settling in her heart like a tiny bird finding a nest.

The only sounds in the kitchen were the soft soughs of their breathing and the low crackle of the fire in the other room. Finally, when she was very much afraid her legs weren't going to support her much longer, Daniel made a sound deep in his throat, something raw and aroused, and deepened the kiss.

She sighed an enthusiastic welcome and returned the kiss. He pulled her closer and she molded her body to his. This time she relished how small and delicate he made her feel next to his size and strength.

They kissed until she couldn't breathe, couldn't think, until she was lost to everything but Daniel, his taste and his scent and his touch.

Suddenly, over the sound of their harsh breathing, she heard something else. The rather prosaic sound of a toilet flushing somewhere in the house. Rosa.

Lauren froze as if she had stepped naked into that storm outside the windows. Jarred back into her senses, she scrambled away from him, her heart beating wildly.

What, in heaven's name, just happened here?

Had she really just been wrapped around *Daniel Galvez?*

Her face flamed and it was all she could do not to press her hands to her cheeks. What must he think of her? She had responded to him like some wild, sex-starved coed. She had all but dragged him to the floor and had her way with him.

She was fairly certain she had even moaned his name a time or two. How could she ever look him in the eye again?

"Rosa must be awake," she said, keeping her gaze firmly in the vicinity of his chest, until she realized that probably wasn't the greatest idea since it only made her want to smooth her hands over those hard muscles once more.

"Sounds like," he said. Did his voice sound more hoarse than usual? she wondered.

She finally risked a look at him and could have sworn he had a dazed kind of look in his eyes—the same baffled, disoriented expression she saw in patients with mild concussions.

Had Daniel been as affected as she had by that shattering kiss? How was it possible? He disliked her. Okay, *dislike* might be a bit harsh. But he certainly never seemed interested in her on that kind of level.

Except once, she reminded herself—so long ago, it seemed another lifetime. More than a decade ago, he had asked her out and she turned him down. Quite firmly, if she recalled.

He had been the first guy to show any interest in her since the grim events of that spring and she had been far too raw and messed-up to even consider it. The very idea had terrified her. The details were a little hazy but she was fairly certain she hadn't been very subtle with her refusal, either.

In all those years, Daniel had never given her any indication he might be interested in her. Things between them were always strained, always slightly uncomfortable, though both of them did their best to be polite.

That kiss, though.

That was certainly not the way an un-interested man kissed a woman.

Her stomach muscles fluttered and she didn't know what to think. She suddenly was desperate for a little space to figure out what had just happened between them.

Distance from the man was not something she would likely find in the next few days, she realized with considerable dismay. Her house was small but had always seemed more cozy than confining to her. With Daniel here—six feet three inches of him and all that muscle—she suddenly felt like the walls were squeezing in, sucking away every particle of oxygen.

"Uh, Lauren—" Daniel began, but whatever he started to say was cut off as Rosa came into the kitchen, looking much more rested than she had when they arrived.

She greeted them with a shy smile, apparently oblivious to the tense undercurrents zinging through the kitchen like hummingbirds on crack cocaine.

"How are you?" Lauren asked in Spanish.

"Better," Rosa answered.

"Sit. I'll get you something to eat. Would you eat some soup?"

She dipped her cheek to her shoulder, looking hesitant to put anyone to more trouble.

Daniel said something in rapid Spanish, too fast for Lauren to understand, and pulled a chair out for her at the table. Rosa's shyness lifted and she giggled a little and nodded, then obediently sat down.

"What did you say?" Lauren asked.

"I told her she had to have some of your delicious soup or I would end up eating it all and end up too fat to wear my uniform."

He gave an embarrassed smile and Lauren stared at it, an odd emotion tugging at her chest.

She was in trouble here, she thought as she hurried to the stove to dish Rosa a bowl of soup. Panic spurted through her and it was all she could do not to drop the soup all over the floor.

Oh, she was in serious trouble.

She could probably handle the physical attraction. But she suddenly realized she had no defenses against a man who had the wisdom to cajole and tease and look after a frightened young girl like she was his own little sister.

The evening that followed had to live on in her memory as one of the most surreal of Lauren's life. While Rosa picked at her bowl of soup, the storm that had been toying with this part of the state all day let loose with a vengeance. The wind lashed snow against the window and moaned under the eaves of her little house.

Daniel threw on his coat and made several trips to the woodpile out back so they had a good supply of split logs close to the house. Lauren gathered lanterns and flashlights just in case the power went out, as it often did during big storms like this that brought heavy, wet snow to knock out power lines.

While she cleaned the kitchen and loaded

the dishwasher, Daniel checked in with his department.

She listened to his strong, confident voice as he reviewed emergency storm protocol with his lieutenant and she thought again how lucky the people of Moose Springs were to have him as their sheriff. He was wonderful at his job and truly cared about the people he served.

She knew her reasons for setting up her practice in her hometown but why did *he* stay here? He could be working anywhere. He had spent his first few years in law enforcement as a Salt Lake City police officer and many had expected him to stay there and make a promising career for himself. Then his mother had fallen ill, his father was killed and he had returned home.

His mother had lost her battle with cancer shortly after Lauren returned to town. So why did Daniel stay all these years?

She enjoyed listening to him. It was silly, she knew, but she loved hearing him in action. Oh, she had it bad.

He ended the phone conversation just as she finished wiping down the countertops.

"If you need to go on a call or something during the night, I'm sure we'll be fine here," Lauren offered.

"I've got good people working for me and I'm sure they have everything under control. But if something comes up that nobody else can handle, one of my deputies can come here and relieve me for a while."

"Does everyone know you're staying at my house?"

His mouth tightened and his expression cooled. It took her a moment to figure out how her question must have sounded, as if she worried about her reputation.

He answered before she could correct the assumption. "No. Only Kurt Banning, my second-in-command, knows the entire story. As far as everybody else is concerned, I'm taking some personal leave. That should set your mind at ease."

"My mind is not at all unsettled."

Not about her reputation, at any rate. She was afraid she had none in Moose Springs.

She could have an entire orgy of sexy law enforcement officers camping at her house and people would just shake their heads and ask what else could they expect of R.J.'s daughter?

"Is there a free plug for my cell phone somewhere?" Daniel asked. "I want to make sure I've got a full charge while I can in case the power goes out on us."

"Yes. Of course. Good idea." She showed him an open plug, then spent a few moments digging out her own cell phone to charge in case she was needed on a medical emergency.

What if they were both called out on a crisis at the same time? she wondered, then decided to set her mind at ease, at least on that score. It was certainly possible, but she had no doubts Daniel would have thought of every eventuality.

The wind lashed the windows as Lauren went to join Rosa in the living area. The girl was curled up on the couch with a blanket over her, watching a comedy on the Spanish language channel. Lauren could only pick out half the words and she was just reaching for her latest lousy attempt at knitting when Daniel joined them and settled in the recliner.

He watched TV with Rosa for ten minutes until the show ended, though she had the feeling he was only pretending to pay attention.

Was he as off balance as she was by that kiss? she wondered. Even a half hour later, she could still taste him on her mouth.

She was wondering if she had any DVDs with Spanish subtitles, for the sake of distraction if nothing else, when Daniel suddenly jumped up from the recliner.

"Let's play a game or something."

"Okay," she said slowly. "What did you have in mind?"

"I don't know. What have you got? You have a deck of cards?"

"I'm sure I do somewhere."

"What about a card table?"

"In the garage against the north wall."

While he went in search of it, she finally unearthed a deck in her kitchen junk drawer that was probably left over from medical school study breaks. While she was searching, Daniel had found the card table and had set it up near the fireplace.

"What did you have in mind?" she asked after the three of them settled into the chairs he brought in from the dining room and he shuffled the deck.

"I don't know. I was trying to come up with some game that would transcend the language thing. What about Crazy Eights?"

She didn't believe she had played that game since she was about ten years old in summer camp. But she was willing to try anything that might keep her mind off that stunning kiss.

For the next hour, they played Crazy Eights and War and SlapJack, and a new one to her called Burro Castigado, similar to draw poker.

Daniel must have been inspired with the cards, Lauren thought. As they played, Rosa giggled and smiled and seemed much more like a girl than a young woman who had survived a horrendous ordeal.

After a while, she moved to the kitchen to make some popcorn and she could overhear Daniel and Rosa speaking in Spanish. Daniel's low laugh drew her gaze.

She watched them together for a moment, a funny pang in her chest. He was so kind to the girl, just as he used to be to his own younger sister. She used to be filled with envy that Anna had three big, strong brothers to watch out for her. It had hardly seemed fair to Lauren, when she had none.

He turned suddenly and caught her watching him. Something flared in his dark eyes, something hot and intense. In her mind, she was in his arms again, savoring that strength around her and the flutter of nerves as her body seemed to awaken from a long, cold sleep.

Their gazes caught for a long moment, until the microwave dinged and yanked Lauren back to reality. She pulled the popcorn bag out and took her time shaking it into a bowl while she tried to force her pulse to slow again. She was never going to make it through the next few days if she didn't get a grip over herself here.

At last she felt in control enough to return to the card table, and pasted on a bright smile.

They played for another half hour, until she caught Rosa trying to cover a yawn. It was nearly eleven, Lauren realized with some surprise.

"You need to sleep," she said to the girl. "Come on, let's get you settled for the night."

Daniel had picked out a warm, roomy nightgown for her and Lauren showed her the toothpaste, washcloths and towels. Rosa bid her good-night with a smile that was growing more relaxed and comfortable.

When she returned to the other room, she found Daniel shrugging into his heavy coat once more.

She frowned. "I'm quite certain you brought

in enough wood earlier to last for at least a week. There is no reason for you to go out into the storm again."

"I figured I'd shovel your walk before I turn in."

She was about to argue the sidewalk could wait until morning but some restless light in his eyes tangled the words in her throat. He looked like a man with energy to burn.

She could think of other ways to exhaust that energy, but she wasn't about to suggest them to him.

"Thank you," she said instead.

She picked up her pitiful knitting again while he was outside and tried to focus on the news, but it was a losing battle. All she could think about was the man out there braving the elements to shovel her sidewalk.

When he returned twenty minutes later, snowflakes were melting in the silky darkness of his hair and his cheeks were flush with cold, but he seemed far easier in his skin.

"It's a b-witch out there," he said, stomping

snow off his boots and shaking it from his coat. "That wind chill coming from the north has got to be at least minus ten. I bet we get a foot or more."

She nodded. "Nights like this make me grateful to be home in front of the fire instead of driving through the snow on my way to an emergency somewhere."

"Makes me glad for insulated windows," he said, shrugging out of his coat. "When I was a kid, we used to stick blankets over all the windows in our house. They were all single-paned. I imagine they probably let in more cold than they kept out."

He laughed suddenly at a memory. "Ren used to put cups of water in front of them so we could measure how long it took for ice to form. He was always doing crazy things like that. First thing I did after I moved back was to replace them all with energy-efficient windows and blow better insulation into the walls. Made a hell of a mess and cost a fortune, but the house stayed about thirty degrees warmer in the winter."

Lauren couldn't help thinking of her own home, where her mother insisted on keeping the thermostat at seventy-three degrees and invariably had a fire going as well. R.J. used to complain about the heat bill, but never enough to make her mother turn down the thermostat.

Of course, her mother didn't know R.J. was heating another house somewhere.

"Would you like something warm?" she asked. "I've got several kinds of cocoa."

His raised eyebrow lifted even higher when she opened a cupboard to show the wide, varied selection inside. Orange chocolate, chocolate raspberry, chocolate mint, chocolate cinnamon, chocolate amaretto and plain old delicious milk chocolate. She had about every flavor of hot chocolate ever invented.

"I'm something of a cocoa junkie in the winter," she admitted ruefully. "Even in the summer sometimes, if I've had a bad day. Nothing comforts quite like it."

He watched her, a strange, unreadable light in his eyes. She didn't know what it meant, she only knew it made those blasted stomach flutters start all over again. After a moment, he shook his head. "Maybe tomorrow night I'll take you up on that."

She let out a breath. However would she endure so much time trapped here in his company, especially when she couldn't stop thinking about that kiss?

"I can help you pull out the couch in the office if you'd like."

"I was just thinking I would stretch out over there, if that's okay with you."

She gazed at the short couch near the fire, then at his long, muscled body. The two things seemed a definite mismatch.

"Are you sure?" she asked. "It's no problem at all to make the couch into a bed."

"This is fine. That way I can be close to keep

the fire going, just in case the storm knocks out the power in the night."

"I'll bring you some blankets and a pillow, then."

She pulled them out of her small linen closet, certain as she returned to the living room that she shouldn't find the idea of him watching over her and Rosa such a comfort.

She was a strong, independent woman. She certainly didn't need a man to take care of her, to bring in her wood and shovel her walks and tend the fire through the night.

She didn't need it, perhaps. But she couldn't deny that she found it very appealing to share the everyday burdens of life with someone else once in a while.

When she returned with the linens, she found him sitting on the recliner, gazing into the fire. He looked up at her entrance, and again she was surprised at the odd, glittery expression in his eyes.

"Here you go. Good night, then. If you need anything else in the night, let me know," she said.

"I'll do that," he murmured, and she could feel the heat of his gaze on her all the way through the kitchen and down the hall to her bedroom.

Chapter 9

Something woke him in the early morning hours.

He instantly sat up, alert and on edge. The house was quiet, the only sound the low murmur of the fire flickering low, reduced now to just a log burned almost all the way through and a few red embers glowing in the dark.

His instincts humming, he looked around, trying to figure out what had awakened him.

The house was *too* dark. *Too* quiet.

It only took a moment for him to figure out why. As he and Lauren had both feared, the power must have gone out in the storm. The fire provided the only light in the house and the usual subtle sounds of a juiced-up house were nowhere in evidence. No buzz of a refrigerator, no whirr of a furnace kicking on. Nothing.

The only thing he could hear now besides the fire was the wind hurling snow at the windows. He slid off the couch and threw another log from the pile onto the glowing embers. It crackled for a moment, but he had no doubt the coals were hot enough that it would soon catch.

Moving with slow caution, he eased to the window and peered out into the storm. He looked up and down her isolated road, but could see no other lights out there, not even the ambient glow from the concentrated lights of town he might have expected.

Though he knew from experience that any power outage was a major pain in the neck for law enforcement officials, the pitch-black set his mind at ease.

If the whole town had lost power, obviously

Lauren's house hadn't been targeted specifically by someone cutting her juice for nefarious reasons.

He didn't know what kind of threat might lurk out there for Rosa, but he wasn't about to take any chances. Someone wanted her dead because of all that she knew. Melodramatic as it seemed, it wasn't wholly out of the realm of possibility that someone might cut Lauren's power to have better access to her house.

They had tried to kill Rosa in her own hospital bed. He had a feeling these bastards would certainly have no qualms about killing anybody else who got in their way.

He hated this whole damn situation. A pretty young girl like Rosa should be dreaming about her *quinceañera*, should be trying out makeup and giggling with her friends and discovering the vast world of possibilities awaiting her. Instead, she was battered and bruised and five months pregnant from a brutal gang rape, doing her best to stay alive.

And Lauren had put herself right in the middle of Rosa's troubles by bringing the girl home to recover.

He sighed, his mind on the woman asleep in her room just a few yards away. What a mess this assignment was turning into. In the first eight hours after bringing Rosa here, he had hurt Lauren's feelings, dredged up memories she didn't want and kissed her until he managed to forget his own name.

He could only wonder, with a strange mix of dread and anticipation, what the morning would bring.

In the soft glow of the fire, he could read the face on his watch. It was 2:30 a.m., which meant he had probably slept a grand total of maybe an hour and a half all night. And though he had slept, he couldn't say those had been the most restful ninety minutes he'd ever enjoyed.

He should have expected it. Lauren's house wasn't exactly conducive to a good night's rest. How could it be, with her subtle scent of jasmine and vanilla surrounding him and the knowledge that she was only a few footsteps away burning in his gut?

He couldn't stop thinking about that kiss, those incredible moments in the kitchen when she had been in his arms, all soft and warm and delicious. After all these years of wondering what it might be like to kiss her, to touch that skin and taste her soft mouth, he had to admit the reality had far surpassed any fantasy.

And reliving the moment over and over again sure as hell wasn't going to help him get any sleep.

He reached for his cell phone and dialed his dispatcher. Tonight, Jay Welch was on duty and as Daniel greeted him, he pitched his voice low so he didn't wake up Lauren or Rosa.

"Hey, Sheriff," Jay said. "I thought you were taking a few nights off, squeezing in a little R and R."

Rest and recreation. Right. There was absolutely nothing remotely restful about staying in

Lauren's house, having to fight like hell to keep his hands off her.

And the only recreation he could seem to wrap his brain around was exactly the activity he knew he wouldn't be engaging in anytime soon.

"I'm still around," he murmured. "Just checking on the situation there with the power out."

"So far, so good. The backup generator kicked in right away. We're starting to get a few anxious calls from people wondering what's going on. The power company says a tree came down north of town and knocked out the power line. They expect to be back in business no later than an hour."

Without electricity, most furnaces couldn't turn on, even if they were natural gas- or oil-fueled. A house could get mighty cold during a January blizzard without heat for an hour. He thought of those single-paned windows in his childhood home and couldn't help a shiver, despite the little fire now burning cheerfully in the grate.

Most people around here had secondary heat sources like fireplaces or wood or pellet stoves, but he didn't want to take any chances with the health and safety of the people of his town. "I'll check in with you in an hour for an update. If it's not back up and running by the time the sun comes up, we're going to want to start welfare checks on some of the senior citizens who live alone."

"Okay."

He hung up and sat on the couch gazing at the dancing flames and wondering what he was supposed to do with all this restlessness burning through him.

Suddenly, he heard a noise somewhere in the house. He reached for his 9mm, thumbed off the safety and rose, alert and ready. An instant later Lauren's bedroom door opened.

She stood just outside the rim of light from the fireplace, but he didn't need illumination to know the sound he heard was her.

He slid the safety on and tucked the gun back

under his pillow on the couch. "I hope I didn't wake you while I was on the phone," he said.

"You didn't. I think I woke when the power went out. That sounds silly, doesn't it?"

"Not *that* silly. I did the same thing."

They lapsed into silence and he wondered why she was out here instead of tucked into her warm bed.

"Everything okay?" he asked.

She stepped farther into the fire's glow and he could see the rueful expression on her face. "I just realized that even after I went to all that trouble to round up secondary light sources for a possible outage, I forgot to take a flashlight into my room when I went to bed. I was lying in bed wondering how I could sneak out here in the dark and grab one without waking you, then I heard you on the phone."

"I was just checking in with dispatch," he said. "Jay Welch has already talked to the power company and we're looking at about an hour before it's back online."

"It's good you had the foresight to keep the fire going," she said, grabbing a flashlight from the table where she had assembled them earlier in the night. "What about Rosa? I wondered if I should let her sleep or wake her to let her know the power is out. I wouldn't want her to wake up in the middle of the night in the pitch-dark and be frightened."

"I can listen for her. If I hear sounds of stirring, I'll explain to her what's going on. Those bedrooms are going to get mighty cold without the furnace if the power company's estimate is wrong and it takes them longer than they figure to fix the problem. I'll have to wake you both up so you can come out here and bunk by the fire where it's warm."

"You don't have to stay up all night to watch over us, Daniel."

"I don't mind."

She tilted her head and studied him and he wondered again what she saw when she looked at him. "I know you don't. You watch over everyone, don't you?"

Is that how she saw him? He shrugged, uncomfortable. "It's my job to keep the people of Moose Springs safe. Go back to bed, try to get some sleep. I'll wake you if the power doesn't come back up in an hour or so."

"I couldn't sleep now anyway."

He should keep his distance from her. One of them should have a little good sense here. If he were smart, he would insist that she march right back into her bedroom and stay away from him.

Too bad he didn't feel very smart around the delectable Dr. Maxwell.

He sighed. "You might as well come in and sit down out here by the fire, then. We can keep each other company until the lights come back on."

She hesitated, just long enough for him to wonder if the tug and pull between them unnerved her as much as it did him. He couldn't have said which he would prefer: that she go back to bed and leave him alone or that she come in and sit beside him so he could indulge his unwilling fascination a little longer.

She chose the second, pausing only long enough to turn on the light switch so they would know when the power was back on, then she sat in the armchair.

In the fire's glow, he could see she wore soft, lace-edged cotton pajamas the color of spring leaves. He did his best not to think about how they would feel under his fingers.

When she pulled her knees up and wrapped her arms around them as if she were cold, he lifted one of the extra blankets she had brought him from the end of the couch and tossed it to her.

"Thanks," she murmured. She snuggled into it, tucking the edges around her feet. They sat for a moment, accompanied only by the low rumble of the fire, their own breathing and the distant wind.

"When I was a kid, I used to love storms like this when the power would go out," she said into the stillness. "That sounds crazy, doesn't it?"

"I guess it depends why you liked it."

"My dad would make it all seem like a big adventure. When the power went out in the middle of the night like this, he would pull out the sleeping bags from the garage and start a fire in the big fireplace in the great room and the three of us would roast marshmallows and pop popcorn and tell stories just like we were camping out."

He had to admit that even after all these years, he didn't like hearing anything positive about R.J. Maxwell. He had never quite understood how a woman like Lauren could come from such a bastard.

"Sounds great," he said politely.

"It was. Even when I was in high school, Dad would still drag us down there. When he was home, anyway. He was always so busy, off on his *business trips*."

The resentment in those last two words left him acutely uncomfortable. He knew the real reason her father spent so much time away from him, but he wasn't sure if *she* knew he was one of the few who were aware of all the facts. They had never talked about this before, about the motives behind R.J.'s embezzlement and everything that went along with it. He wasn't sure he wanted to talk about it now, in the hushed peace of the night.

Before he could come up with a response, she shook her head slightly; and even in the darkened room, he could see regret flitter across her lovely features.

"Sorry. I didn't mean to sound embittered. I really do try not to be, but sometimes it slips through."

"You have a right to be angry, Lauren."

She had a right to be angry at *Daniel,* he thought. She just didn't know it—and he didn't know if he had the courage to tell her.

"Most of the time the whole situation just makes me sad." She gazed into the fire, avoiding Daniel's gaze. "If R.J. hadn't taken a coward's way out of the mess he created, the first question I would ask would have been why my mother and I weren't enough for him."

"He loved you, Lauren. He was always proud of his daughter."

"Right." After a moment she smiled, though it looked strained. "Let's talk about something else, can we? I'm really not in the mood to dredge up any more of the past tonight."

What are you in the mood for? he wanted to ask. The question almost spilled out as images flashed through his mind of those heated moments in her kitchen earlier.

He forced his mind away from that dangerous line of thought. As much as he yearned to taste her and touch her again, he knew it was impossible.

"You want to pick the topic or should I?" he asked after a moment.

Her teeth flashed white in the dark as she smiled. "I will. I was wondering this earlier. What are you doing here, Daniel?"

"W-e-e-ll," he drew out. "It's a little cold sleeping out in my truck on a night like tonight. Your couch is much more comfortable for guard-dog duty."

"I don't mean here, right now. I mean, why did you stick around in Moose Springs? I know you came back to help your mother when she was sick. But after she died, why did you stay here when you could have gone anywhere?"

He hadn't been expecting the question and it took him a moment to formulate a reply. "I don't think there's any one answer to that. This is my home and I love it here. That's one reason, probably the easiest, most obvious one."

"What else?"

"I don't know." He shrugged. "Maybe I felt like I had something to prove."

Her eyes widened with surprise. "Why would you think that?"

"We grew up in different worlds, Lauren."

"Not that different. You lived three blocks away."

"In a shack that R.J. probably wouldn't have considered a fit place to store his riding mower."

In the glow from the fire, she looked flushed. "Your parents were wonderful people. Your mother was always so sweet. Every kid in town would save their allowance for weeks to buy those cherry empanadas she sold at Moose-mania Days. And I don't think I ever saw your father when he wasn't smiling."

"I agree. They were great people. That didn't change the fact in a lot of people's minds that we were dirt-poor Mexicans."

As soon as the words were out, he heartily wished he hadn't said them. He didn't need to emphasize the differences between them. They were obvious enough.

"And so you wanted to show people you were more than that. That's why you worked so hard in school, why you pushed yourself at football, why you worked to become an indispensable deputy in the sheriff's office?"

"It started out that way, anyhow. Pretty pathetic, isn't it?"

"You had nothing to prove, Daniel. Absolutely nothing! Look at all you've achieved! Not only did you have a full-on football scholarship, but you were the high school valedictorian, as I recall, and Ren was the year after you. Anna would have had the same honor in our grade but, uh, someone else beat her to it. She had to settle for salutatorian."

"Don't worry. She doesn't hold a grudge against you. At least not much of one."

She laughed, as he had hoped she would. It echoed softly through the room and warmed him at least a dozen degrees.

"I don't know about Marcos, since he was a few years behind Anna and me. How were his grades?"

"He was third in the class."

"What a slacker!"

"We think it's because he was the baby and Mom and Dad took it easier on him than the rest of us."

She smiled, then tilted her head to study him. "You're a good sheriff, Daniel. Maybe the best Moose Springs has ever had."

He fought the urge to rub an embarrassed

hand to the burn at the back of his neck. "I don't know about that. I can say, I never expected to enjoy it as much as I do. Being here, being home, feels right."

"Think you'll ever move away?"

"I don't know. I get offers once in a while. But it all comes back to me asking myself if I could really be happy anywhere else. I don't have a good answer to that so for now I'm staying."

"Good." She spoke barely above a whisper and the sound of her low voice strummed down his spine like a soft caress. His gaze met hers and she didn't look away.

Again, the memory of that kiss seemed to shimmer between them and he could think of nothing else, the sound of her murmuring his name when he kissed her, the taste of her as she opened for him, warm and welcoming, how perfectly *right* she had seemed in his arms.

He wanted more. Much, much more.

He could kiss her again. He knew it wouldn't take much for him to lean forward and close the distance between them. The ache to touch her again was a physical burn in his gut.

Even as he started to lean forward, to take what he so desperately wanted, reality came rushing in like that cold wind out there and froze his muscles.

Things were tense enough between them. Was he willing to throw in another kiss that could never lead anywhere?

Yeah.

Hell, yeah.

But he wasn't sure where things stood between them. Though she responded the last time in the heat of the moment, she had looked stunned afterward and he was certain he had caught more than a glimmer of dismay in her gaze.

He let out a breath and the sound of it seemed to echo in the still room. "Lauren—" he began, not sure what he intended to say. *Kiss me before I die on the spot,* maybe.

Whatever it might have been was driven from his mind when the power came back on suddenly, an abrupt, jarring shift from dim to full, bright light.

He blinked a few times to adjust his vision. When he could see through the glare, he saw that in those brief moments she had drawn her arms tighter around her knees and all her defenses were firmly in place.

Just as well. The seductive intimacy of those few moments alone in the dark with her could never survive the harsh glare of light.

She was relieved, Lauren told herself firmly. The power switching back on at just that moment when he had been gearing up to kiss her—and she had so desperately wanted him to—must have been some kind of an omen, a karmic warning that she was messing in dangerous things she damn well ought to stay clear of.

She might be able to sell that argument to her intellect. Her body was another matter entirely, and all she seemed able to focus on now was the deep well of disappointment inside her.

The furnace kicked in and she knew it would be blowing its warmth through the house any moment now.

"Looks like we're back in business," she murmured, mostly to fill the sudden awkward void between them.

"For now. Let's hope it stays on."

She shouldn't regret the loss of that quiet intimacy between them. She knew it was dangerous, knew it filled her mind with all sorts of treacherous thoughts, but she couldn't help feeling as if she had lost something rare, something precious.

"I suppose I'll say good night, then."

"Try to get some rest."

"Same to you."

She rose, self-conscious now about her favorite threadbare pajamas. She hadn't given them a thought when the power was out, but now she wished she'd thrown a robe on before wandering out.

In her bedroom, she closed the door behind her and leaned against it, just for a moment.

It was foolish, she knew, but she wanted the electricity to blink out again. She wanted to be sitting out there with Daniel in the dim firelight, to be listening to his deep voice and feeling the strength and heat of him. A few more moments. Was that too much to ask?

Too bad she had learned the bitter lesson long ago that a girl couldn't always have everything she wanted.

Chapter 10

Two days later, Lauren was just about ready to climb out of her skin. She was beginning to understand the frustrated restlessness of a mouse in a cage.

After forty-eight hours in her house with only Daniel and Rosa, she was edgy and out of sorts and needed some sort of physical outlet. If the snow wasn't still howling out there, she would suit up and jog around the block. The idea tempted her, despite the blizzard, but she decided she really wasn't in the mood for the inevitable argument with Daniel about it.

She had to settle for the mild but distracting exertion of cooking dinner for the three of them.

Not wanting to bother Rosa and Daniel in the adjoining room, she tried her best not to bang pots and pans around as she pulled out the frying pan she needed to sauté chicken.

They didn't even look up from their movie as she set it on the stove and added olive oil to begin heating.

They were watching a DVD of a comedy with Spanish subtitles and every once in a while she could hear their laughter echo through the little house. She was pleased to hear Rosa relaxing, but each time she heard Daniel's bass laugh, she felt as if he had reached across the distance between them to stroke her neck with strong fingers.

Outside, the wind continued to lash snow against the window, as it had much of the day. The blizzard had continued on and off for two days and Daniel had been on the phone a great deal, coordinating his department's response to the storm.

She didn't find much consolation that this enforced isolation was tough on him as well, especially in the midst of a weather crisis. Some time ago, she tried to convince him she and Rosa would be fine here alone for a few hours if he needed to get out in the middle of the action with his deputies.

She thought it had been a reasonable enough suggestion. Daniel just raised one of those expressive eyebrows of his and assured her he wasn't going anywhere.

More's the pity. She sighed as she finished cutting up a chicken breast and slid it into the olive oil in the frying pan, filling the kitchen with sizzling heat.

Maybe he would let *her* go somewhere and help his department with the storm cleanup. True, she didn't know a blasted thing about directing traffic or cleaning up weather-caused accidents. But at this point, she was just about willing to do anything that would get her out of the house for a moment or two so she could regain a little psychic equilibrium.

She filled her large stockpot with water for the pasta, then set it on to boil while she tackled the fresh vegetables for another of her few specialties. She was slicing red and yellow peppers when Daniel laughed again at something on the show.

A shiver slid through her and she almost chopped her finger off. Oh, this was ridiculous. Still, she couldn't resist a quick peek into the other room. Rosa was stretched out on the couch while Daniel had taken over Lauren's favorite easy chair. He sprawled in it, wearing jeans and a rust-colored sweater. He looked rugged and masculine and so gorgeous, he made her insides ache.

She was in serious trouble here.

She grabbed the onion and started slicing it fiercely. Her eyes started watering profusely, but she didn't care. Damn him, anyway. For two days, she had done her best to ignore the thick tension between them, but she wasn't making any progress whatsoever.

He was just so…*there.* He seemed to fill every corner of her small house with the potent force of his personality.

She found everything about him fascinating. She enjoyed listening to him talk to his deputies with a firm voice that managed to convey authority and respect at the same time. She liked watching him with Rosa. He treated the bruised and battered girl with a gentle kindness that touched her deeply.

She also admired his deep reservoir of patience, this further proof that he was often quite literally the quiet spot in a storm to those around him. For a man with such an overwhelming personality, Daniel had an almost Zen-like calmness to him in the middle of a crisis.

Calm did not mean *detached.* Not in the least. Even now, when he appeared relaxed and at ease watching a movie, he never seemed to shed that subtle air of alertness about him, like some kind of predator constantly sniffing the air for prey.

Throughout the last two days, he had put on his winter gear several times to brave the storm, ostensibly to shovel the driveway or for more firewood, but she had the feeling he also used the opportunity to case her house and its surroundings, looking for anything unusual.

He was a dangerous man, she thought as she stirred the chicken. More so, she imagined, because it would be easy—and disastrous—for an opponent to mistake his outward calm for inward placidity. Anyone foolish enough to err so badly would have to overlook those sharp dark eyes that never seemed to miss anything.

She could only hope they didn't see *everything*. She would die of mortification if he guessed her attraction.

Oh, she had it bad. Now that it was out in the open in her psyche, she couldn't believe she had missed it all these years, all the reasons she was tense and uncomfortable around him.

Her attraction had always been this undefined thing in her mind, this awareness of him that was somehow lost in her frustration and sadness over the past.

How would their relationship change after this time with Rosa was over? How on earth could things ever return to the way they were before, that wary but polite accord?

She was checking the cookie sheet of bread-sticks baking in the oven, their yeasty smell mingling with the spices in the chicken, when some sixth sense warned her Daniel had entered the kitchen behind her.

Even without turning around, she knew he was there by a sudden subtle vibration in the air, a stirring of the molecules, an alertness in her nerve endings.

Her pulse kicked up a notch, as it seemed to do whenever he was within five feet of her, but she pasted on a smile and turned around, only to find him watching her with an odd expression on his face, something dark and intense and unsettling.

He hid it quickly and moved to the coffeepot to refill his cup. "Smells delicious," he said, gesturing to the sizzling chicken. Did he sound more gruff than usual? she wondered, then dismissed the thought.

"Thanks," she murmured.

"You don't have to do all the cooking. I know we've talked about this but I should have been more proactive. Sorry to dump the burden on you. Things have been a little crazy, with the storm and all. To be honest, I forgot all about it, but I promise, I'll cook breakfast and dinner tomorrow."

"I really don't mind cooking," she assured him.

"It's only fair. And I don't mind it, either."

"Do you expect you and Rosa will still be here by dinnertime tomorrow?" she asked.

"I'm still waiting to hear from Cale on the status of their safe house situation. We'll know better after he checks in." He paused. "Whenever we get out of here, I imagine you'll be happy to have us out of your way."

"You're not in my way."

Much.

She was a lousy liar and his rueful half smile indicated he didn't believe her any more than she believed herself.

Not that she would be completely thrilled to have them gone. On the one hand, she would be vastly relieved when her life returned to normal and her clinic reopened. On the other, she was terribly afraid she would be lonely when this was all over.

She had a good life, she reminded herself as she added the pasta to the boiling water. Every day she tried to make a difference in the world, to help the people of her community live healthier, happier lives. She had no reason at all for this discontent simmering under her skin.

"You know," he said after a moment, "if Cale and McKinnon do find another placement for Rosa in the next day or two, you would still have time left of your vacation to go visit your mom in southern Utah."

"Maybe. I don't want to make any definite plans until things are figured out here."

The timer went off, indicating the breadsticks were done. She slid them out, aware of him watching her the whole time.

"Anything I can do in here?"

She wanted him out of the kitchen. How could she possibly concentrate on cooking with him crowding her psyche this way? "No. I just need to toss it all together. Go back to your movie. Everything should be ready in ten minutes or so."

"I can set the table, at least."

"All right."

For the next few moments, they worked together in silence, Daniel setting out plates and silverware while Lauren brushed melted butter on the breadsticks and finished sautéing the vegetables.

She was concentrating so fiercely on trying to ignore him that she nearly caused a disaster. When she determined the pasta was done, she carried the stockpot to the sink to drain and almost collided with Daniel, who must have gone to the cupboard by the sink for glasses.

He caught her and steadied her, but a tiny amount of hot liquid spilled over onto the front of his sweater.

"I'm sorry!" she exclaimed. "Are you all right?"

"Fine. It's a thick sweater."

This time she was certain his voice sounded rough. She lifted her gaze from his shirtfront to his face and that jumpy, fluttery feeling twirled through her insides at the raw hunger she surprised in his expression.

"I... Good," she said breathlessly. They froze there in an awkward tableau, then he stepped away.

"You'd better drain that before you get burned."

The pasta. Right. She hurried to the sink, hoping he would attribute her sudden flush to the cloud of steam curling around her.

The doorbell rang just as the three of them were clearing the dinner dishes. The change in

Daniel was rapid and disconcerting. One moment he was teasing Rosa in Spanish, the next he became alert, predatory.

"Stay here," he ordered, his voice hard and flat.

He headed toward the door, reaching for something under his sweater. He had a gun. Good Lord. She should have realized he would be armed. He was here for protection, for heaven's sake, she reminded herself. He couldn't very well face down Gilberto Mata with nothing but his fists, no matter how powerful they were.

Still, the sight of that stark, black weapon in his hand drove home the precariousness of the situation—and the dangerous edge to Daniel's nature he usually managed to cloak from view.

From the angle of the kitchen cabinets, she only had a sliver of a view into the entryway. She watched Daniel ease to the front window and barely twitch the curtains to look out on to the porch, just like a gunfighter in the Wild West.

She held her breath, but whatever he saw

there must have set his mind at ease. He quickly holstered his weapon again and worked the locks on the door.

"It's okay. Everything's okay." She gave a Rosa a reassuring smile when she heard Daniel greeting Cale Davis.

A moment later, both men entered her kitchen, and the cozy room instantly seemed to shrink. Though Lauren knew Rosa had met the FBI agent when she was in the hospital, the girl seemed tense and anxious in his presence.

Seeing her reaction only reinforced to Lauren how very comfortable Rosa had become with Daniel. That thought was further validated when Daniel smiled at Rosa and she visibly relaxed.

"We've just finished eating," Lauren said. "There's plenty left. Are you hungry?"

He shook his head. "I'm fine, thanks. Megan's holding dinner for me at home so I can't stay long. Since your place is on my way home, I figured I would stop and see how things have been going."

"Quiet," Daniel answered.

"That's good. Just the way we like it. Sorry I haven't checked in with you before now. We've been in the middle of a big bust on another case. I think we've finally tied up all those loose ends and are ready to put all our energies into this case."

"Has there been any progress?" Lauren asked.

Cale glanced quickly at Rosa, who was hovering close to Daniel. "Some," he said. "We're closing in on the smuggling ring. With the information Rosa gave us, we've been able to find Gilberto Mata. We know who he is and we've got a tail on him."

"Have you arrested him?"

Cale shook his head. "Not yet. We're trying to track his movements, his known associates, that kind of thing, to see if we can figure out who else might be involved and find the other girls Rosa talked about. Her friend and the others. That's going to take some time. We know from her statement that she knows at least four other men were involved besides Mata, the three other men who raped her and who handled the day-to-day operations and another one who seemed to be calling the shots. There have got to be more than that if they're keeping the other girls somewhere—"

Rosa said something quickly in Spanish to Daniel, a questioning look on her fragile, half-healed features. She must have been asking him to translate the conversation. Since Lauren had spent the last two days trying in vain to follow the rapid conversations between Rosa and Daniel, she thought she understood how Rosa felt.

"Can I tell her what you said? She deserves to know what's going on," Daniel said.

Cale pursed his lips. "You're right. She does."

Daniel quickly explained what the agent had said and Rosa nodded. Lauren actually understood her response as she asked him in Spanish why they hadn't already arrested the man who hurt her.

Cale apparently understood some Spanish as well. "Explain to her that we can't move too quickly on this and risk blowing the whole in-vestigation by sending them all running back over the border. As I said, we're still trying to find the other girls she talked about. We need a few more days to make sure we can get them out safely when this all goes down."

Daniel translated his words to Rosa, who nodded solemnly.

"Federal prosecutors want to convene a grand jury by Tuesday or Wednesday so we can get some indictments. We would like to prep Rosa to testify as early as the day after that."

He looked at Lauren. "Do you think she'll be up to that?"

"Are you asking me as her doctor or as her friend?" she asked, and couldn't help the ri-diculous little glow that blossomed inside her when Daniel gave her a wide smile of approval.

"Both, I suppose," Cale answered.

"I think you're going to need to ask her that. Medically, there's no reason she can't testify. She's rebounding remarkably well from a horrific beating. She still has pain and will for some time, but both she and the baby seem to be fine. Emotionally, she's suffered months of trauma and she's going to be healing from that for a long time."

Cale turned to the girl and asked her in Spanish if she would be willing to testify about what happened to her so the men who hurt her could be arrested.

She shook her head vehemently, her eyes wide and her expression taut with fear. Lauren instinctively went to her. But Daniel moved first. He squeezed her shoulder gently and spoke in a soft, reassuring voice.

At first, Lauren couldn't understand what he said. Only after she translated the words in her mind did his meaning become clear. He told Rosa she was strong and beautiful, courageous enough to handle this task they put before her, as hard as it would be, and he swore he would be with her the entire way.

Rosa swallowed hard, her fingers trembling

as she twisted them together. She looked as if she wanted to run out the door and escape this whole situation, but after a moment she seemed to straighten her shoulders.

"If it will help the other girls to be safe and away from those bad men, then yes, I will tell what I know."

Daniel smiled at her with pride and affection. As Lauren gazed at those strong, handsome features, the terrifying truth poured over her like someone had just rushed into the kitchen and dumped a bucket full of snow over her head.

She was in love with him.

Instinctively, she fought to deny it. She couldn't be. It wasn't possible.

Yes, she was attracted to him. That was a normal physiological reaction to a powerful, gorgeous man. Yes, she admired his dedication and his commitment to his job and his town, his kindness and his compassion.

But *love*.

That was something else entirely.

Even as her mind tried to rationalize, to frantically search for some escape, the inevitable truth seemed to settle into her chest, seeping into her soul.

She was in love with Daniel Galvez.

How could she have missed it all these years? They had definitely been there, these feelings growing inside her. Looking back, she could see clear signs. She had always had a bit of a crush on him as a girl—just like all the other girls at school.

Daniel had been tall, dark, gorgeous, athletic—and slightly rough around the edges. All the things that twittered the hearts of silly teenage girls, and she had been no different.

She had put it out of her mind over the years, but since they both returned to Moose Springs as adults and she watched the kind of man that boy had grown into, these tender feelings had been growing inside her—untended and wild, but still somehow finding root.

Through her dismay, she realized Cale and Daniel were still talking about the case.

"What about the safe-house situation?" Daniel asked.

"We should have everything set by tomorrow afternoon. We've got a couple female agents standing ready to stay with her. One of them is fluent in Spanish, too."

"That's good," Daniel said, relief in his voice. "I'll feel better if she has someone to talk to."

"Things will be easier with her in our place by the U. This way the prosecutors will have easier access to prep her for her testimony." Cale paused. "You two okay here one more night?"

"I'm good," Daniel said. "Lauren?"

No. She was *not* good. Didn't anybody else notice the sane order of her life crumbling around her feet?

"She can stay here as long as necessary," she managed.

"Thanks. Tomorrow should be sufficient."

Could she make it through one more day?

she wondered as Daniel showed Cale to the door and she and Rosa resumed clearing the dishes from the kitchen table.

Oh, this was a complete disaster, she thought as she stood filling the sink with soapy water for the dishes that weren't dishwasher-safe. She was destined for heartache here.

She thought of the tension that was always there just below the surface when she was with Daniel. He didn't share her feelings. She had never picked up any kind of vibe like that.

Maybe she just missed it. She had been too stupid to realize her own feelings. But he had kissed her.

A fluke, she assured herself, a temporary aberration brought on by the heat and intensity of the moment.

Who would have guessed when she stepped up to offer a wounded patient a sanctuary for a few days that she would discover a grim truth about herself that would rock her to the core?

"Everything okay?"

She looked up from the sink to find Daniel had returned to the kitchen and was watching her with concern in his eyes.

"Much harder and you're going to scrub the nonstick coating right out of that pan," he said.

She stilled her movements, hoping the truth wasn't painfully obvious in her features.

"Yes. Of course. Everything's fine," she lied. "Just fine. Why wouldn't it be?"

Chapter 11

Something was wrong.

Daniel covertly studied Lauren throughout the remainder of the evening, trying to figure out exactly what had happened at dinnertime to make her so jumpy and out of sorts.

She tried to hide it, but he could see some kind of turmoil seething in her blue eyes. Though she went through the motions of watching another DVD with them, he didn't think she caught any of it. Half the time she wasn't even looking at the screen, she was gazing into the flickering fire or out the window at the snow. She seemed the proverbial million miles away.

Maybe this situation was harder on her than she let on. *He* sure as hell found it a nightmare.

Being this close to Lauren—living in her house, surrounded by her things, by her scent, by her sheer presence—was just about the hardest assignment he had ever endured.

He had gone undercover as a scumbag drug dealer for five months back on the job in Salt Lake City and had seen—and done—things that still made his gut burn. All for the greater good of busting up a crime ring that focused exclusively on hooking junior high and high school kids on methamphetamines.

The whole thing had been a miserable, soul-sucking time in his life. While the two dozen resulting arrests hadn't completely washed away the stink of it from his skin, they had certainly helped.

Sitting in Lauren's house, pretending a casualness he was far from feeling, seemed much harder than those five months.

He ached to touch her again. Every time he came within a few feet of her, he had to shove his hands in his pockets to keep from reaching for her.

Maybe that's why she was so twitchy, because she feared he was going to jump her again any minute now.

She didn't need to worry. He could have reassured her on that score. He had vowed to himself the night before that he would keep his hands off her for the duration of this assignment and he would damn well keep that oath, no matter how impossible it seemed at times.

The music on the movie swelled and he realized the closing credits were rolling. He hadn't paid much more attention than Lauren. He only hoped Rosa had enjoyed it.

"Do you want to watch another one?" Lauren asked in Spanish.

Rosa shook her head. "I'm tired," she said softly, her hand resting on her abdomen.

Lauren studied her with concern. "You're hurting, aren't you?"

Rosa started to deny it, then finally she shrugged.

Lauren turned to him. "Can you ask her if it would be all right for me to check her temperature and blood pressure? I'm afraid I don't quite have the language skills."

He repeated her question to Rosa, who shrugged again. She *did* look achy and upset and he admired Lauren's powers of observation.

She rose with her usual grace and left the room. When she returned, she carried her medical bag. She flipped up the lights they had dimmed for the movie and sat down next to Rosa on the couch.

As usual, he found watching Dr. Maxwell in action far more absorbing than anything on the silver screen. Despite her halting Spanish, she made Rosa completely comfortable with her quiet skill. After a quick check of temperature and blood pressure, she pulled out a small sensor from her bag, the same one she had used during her initial exam of Rosa.

"I'm going to check the baby's heartbeat, okay?" She patted her chest to pantomime a heart beating and pointed at Rosa's abdomen.

"Do you want me to leave?" Daniel asked.

"That's up to Rosa."

He repeated the question to the girl, who shook her head. "Just turn around," Rosa ordered.

He had to smile at the peremptory tone— something she was using more and more as she became more comfortable with them both. He complied, then was astonished a moment later to hear a rapid, steady heartbeat filling the room.

"Is that the baby?" he asked, amazed at the strength of it.

"That's her," Lauren said. "She's a fighter. That's a strong, normal heartbeat."

A moment later, the miraculous sound stopped. "You can turn around now," Lauren said.

When he shifted his gaze, he saw she was

putting the monitor thingie away while Rosa pulled her shirt back down. Instead of looking thrilled to hear the heartbeat, she was looking increasingly distressed.

Lauren must have picked up on it, too. "What is it?"

Rosa shrugged but her chin gave an ominous quiver and her big dark eyes started to fill up with tears.

Daniel's first instinct—like that of any sane man—was to shove his chair back and run like hell. Lauren could handle it. She must know exactly how to deal with a young girl's tears.

She'd been one, after all.

He started to shift his weight forward to escape, but Lauren caught the movement. She impaled him in place with a glare.

"What is it? Everything is fine. Good. Are you hurting somewhere else?" she asked in her stilted Spanish.

He sighed. As much as he desperately wanted to escape any emotional outburst, he couldn't leave, not with the language barrier between Lauren and her patient.

Rosa pressed a hand to her chest. "Here," she said.

"You're having chest pains?" In her dismay, Lauren forgot herself and asked the question in English, then looked helplessly at him. He repeated the question in Spanish.

Rosa sniffled once, and then unleashed the floodgates. "My heart," she sobbed. "It aches inside me. I worry so much. What will happen to my baby? She did nothing wrong and I do not want her to die. I am glad she is a fighter, as Dr. Lauren says, that Gilberto Mata did not kill her. But I cannot love her. Who will take care of her?"

Daniel couldn't begin to imagine what she must be going through, pregnant as a result of rape, afraid for her life in a country where she didn't speak the language.

"What did she say?" Lauren demanded, frustration at the language barrier obvious in her features.

"She's worried about the baby."

"Her heartbeat was fine. Better than fine. It's great," Lauren said, clearly baffled.

"Not the baby's physical well-being. More about what will happen to her." He translated the rest of what Rosa had said and watched the anxiety in Lauren's eyes turn to soft compassion.

"Oh, Rosa," she said, and hugged the girl. *Big help there,* he thought, panicking more. Rosa only seemed to sob harder.

After a tense moment, she seemed to calm down and Lauren produced a tissue.

"The other day in the hospital, you said you wanted to give the baby up for adoption, remember? Rosa, there are wonderful couples with so much love to give a child. If that's what you decide, we will find the perfect home for your baby, I promise you. I'll help you. You can choose exactly where the baby goes."

He translated for Lauren, though he had the impression the girl understood the gist.

She twisted the tissue in her hands until it was mangled. "But what if my baby hates me for giving her away?"

"She won't. I promise." She squeezed the girl's hands, tissue and all. "I can tell you that from experience. I was adopted and I have never been anything but grateful to the woman who gave me life."

He stared at her, struck dumb at that unexpected bit of information. How had he never known that about her, in all his months of investigating R.J.? Or maybe he had learned it, he had just been so consumed with vengeance he hadn't internalized the information.

He suddenly remembered his translator duties and relayed what she had said to Rosa. Her words seemed to ease much of the girl's worries. Lauren spent a few more moments reassuring her, until the tears appeared to have dried up, to his vast relief.

"Come on," Lauren said. "The best thing for

you right now is rest. You will feel much better about everything in the morning."

"Thank you," Rosa whispered. "Thank you for everything. You have both been so kind to me."

Lauren hugged her once more, then went with her to help settle her for the night.

She returned just as Daniel was throwing another log on the fire. She paused inside the room and again he caught the wild edge of restlessness in her stance.

"I don't believe I ever knew you were adopted," he said.

She blinked as if she hadn't quite been expecting his statement. "It wasn't some big dark secret," she said. "I don't think about it much, it's just part of who I am."

"What were the circumstances?"

"The usual, I guess. My parents were married for five years and found out they couldn't conceive. This was in the early days of in vitro. They tried everything, apparently, without success. Finally they went the private adoption route."

"Do you know anything about your birth mother?"

"Only that she was young and pregnant and alone, like Rosa," she said. "That's all."

Was this the reason Rosa's situation seemed to affect Lauren so strongly? She had sympathized with the girl from the very beginning. He had asked her why she had insisted on bringing Rosa home with her to Moose Springs to heal. Perhaps this helped explain her actions somewhat.

"She chose my parents before the birth," Lauren continued, "but stipulated there be no contact between them. My mother and father never met her. I don't know anything more about her than that."

"Have you ever wanted to look for her?"

"When I was in high school, I was curious. I guess I grew out of it, right around the time I figured out only fools go borrowing trouble."

"How do you know it would be trouble?" he asked. "Maybe you would be friends."

"Maybe. I just figured she could find me if she wanted. She knew my parents' names and where they lived. She would only have to Google R.J.'s name to know the whole ugly story. It wouldn't be hard to find mention of his only surviving child in those stories. His only legal one, anyway."

Again, he heard the bitterness in her voice. He knew the reason for it and he ached for her. Before he could respond, she spoke again.

"We don't need to dance around this, Daniel. You must know all the gory details. You worked in the sheriff's department at the time everything happened so I'm sure you were privy to all the juicy details that never made it into the papers."

If she only knew.

Before he could respond, Lauren forced a smile. "I'm sure you're wondering if my mother's inability to conceive had anything to do with the choices R.J. made later. The other family he kept in Salt Lake City. His three bouncing baby boys from another woman who thought she was happily married to a man who merely traveled more than she liked. I've certainly wondered the same thing. My mother was unable to give him a son and apparently he found someone who could."

Though she tried to hide it, he heard the raw pain in her voice and would have given anything to have the right words to ease it, as she had comforted Rosa.

"I do know the truth," he said carefully. "But you can be sure I'm one of only a few who do."

"I figured as much, otherwise everyone in town would know by now."

"Have you met them?"

She gave a humorless laugh. "Still more trouble I didn't want to go borrowing. My family tree is quite a wild tangle, isn't it? But yes, I have met my half brothers. Ian, Jamie and Kevin. And their mother. She's a very sweet woman who didn't deserve a betrayal like this."

"Neither did you or your mother."

"No, we didn't." She sighed. "I'm sorry. You must think I brood about the past constantly. I've talked about this more the last few days than I have since it all happened. I'm not sure why that is, but I would really like to put it behind me."

This was the perfect opening for him to tell her the truth he had been running from, the guilt that burned through him whenever they talked about the grim ghosts of the past.

He hesitated. If he told her, everything between them would be ruined, this fragile friendship that had begun to take flight the last few days. If he told her, she would loathe him. How could she not?

Perhaps he would be better to just let things stay as they were. No. He couldn't take the coward's way out, not about this.

He sighed. He had to come clean, and damn the consequences.

"Lauren, there's something I should tell you."

* * *

She studied him across the room, his darkly handsome features suddenly solemn, and her stomach jumped with nerves.

"Whatever it is, I don't want to hear it," she said immediately, jumping up from her chair. "Not tonight."

"Lauren—"

She cut him off. "I need to do something physical. If you need anything, I'll be in my room on my yoga mat in the downward-facing dog."

He studied her intently, until she flushed under the weight of it. She could only hope he couldn't see the wild chaos of emotions she was doing her best to hide from him.

"Why are you running away?" he asked.

"Who's running away?" she retorted, then sighed at his raised eyebrow. "Okay," she admitted. "I'm running away."

"Why?"

She gave a short laugh. "I'm a physician, Daniel. In my world *we need to talk* is just about the most terrible thing I can say to a patient. The only time I ever use those words, I invariably follow them up with something really awful. Whatever it is you want to tell me about my father or anything else, I don't want to hear it. Not tonight. I don't care if that makes me some kind of an ostrich up to my eyeballs in sand. I just...I can't take any more right now."

Though she knew it was rude to a guest in her home, she left without waiting for an answer and retreated to her bedroom, where she quickly changed into workout clothes.

At first, she pushed herself through her asanas, but after ten minutes or so her body and mind relaxed and she could feel the long days of tension begin to seep out of her.

Thirty-five minutes later, she finished her usual poses and was asking herself why she hadn't tried this days ago to still the turmoil inside her, when she heard the outside door open and close.

Daniel must be outside shoveling snow, she

assumed. This would probably be the perfect time for her to grab a bottled water from the refrigerator, something she had neglected earlier in her haste to escape from him.

For the first time in days, her mind wasn't churning and her muscles felt pleasantly loose as she went to the kitchen and opened the refrigerator. She found a bottle and was taking a long, refreshing drink when that sixth sense warned her she wasn't alone.

She turned and found Daniel standing in the doorway, his eyes shadowed.

Her relaxed feeling disappeared. Acutely conscious of her yoga clothes—a midriff-baring tank and stretchy capris—she swallowed hard, sincerely wishing she had never left her mat.

"Snow's stopped."

Her nerves tingled at the hoarse note in his voice.

"I… Good. That's good."

"I'd say we got at least a foot out of the storm. Maybe eighteen inches."

How could he possibly talk about the weather, with all the currents zinging between them? She couldn't even manage to string together a coherent thought.

"How'd the, er, low-down dog go?"

That strange note in his voice caught her attention again and she took a closer look at his expression. She finally saw the hunger there—hot desire with an edge of desperation.

She continued to stare at him, hypnotized by the twitch of muscle in his jaw. He was so big, so dangerously male, and all she could think about was how easy it would be to tug him into her bedroom right now and get her hands on all that hard strength.

He wanted her. She couldn't quite believe it, but she couldn't deny the evidence in his eyes.

"It's the, um, downward-facing dog." Her voice sounded hoarse as well. "I feel much better—all loose and relaxed. You should try it."

She took another swallow from the bottled water. When she lowered it, she found him staring at her mouth. Had she left a water droplet or two there? she wondered, sweeping her tongue across her bottom lip to be sure.

Daniel made a strangled sound. "You're killing me here, Lauren."

"I'm…what?"

"I have to kiss you again. I'm sorry."

She had only half a second to wonder why he seemed compelled to apologize for something she wanted with a fierce ache, and then she was in his arms.

His lips were cold from being outside and he tasted of mint. She shivered as he pressed her against the cabinet, his mouth hard and possessive. Oh, my. She wrapped her arms around his neck, relishing the strength of him against her curves. Raising her arms lifted her exercise tank another few inches, baring more of her midriff and she could feel the nubby texture of his sweater against her skin.

When he slid a hand to her bare back, under the cotton of her tank, and pulled her closer, she forgot all about it—forgot to breathe or think or do anything but exist in the heat of his arms. Raw sensation glittered through at the touch of his fingers on her bare skin, at his tongue stroking hers.

Oh, my.

He was so big and solid, like those mountains outside the window, and she wanted to melt into him.

Where their kiss two days before had been slow, easy as a sluggish creek on a hot summer day, this one was a raging, churning whirlpool. She feared if she wasn't careful, the urgent force of it would suck her down and carry her away.

Clinging wildly to the spinning edges of her sanity, she summoned every ounce of willpower and managed to wrench her mouth away from his long enough to come up for air.

She could feel his chest's rapid rise and fall, see the dazed desire in his eyes.

Had she really done that to him? It didn't seem possible that she could have that effect on someone who was usually so calm and unruffled under any circumstances.

"You taste just like I always imagined you would," he murmured.

It took a moment for his words to sink in. When they did, she raised disbelieving eyes to his. "You…imagined kissing me?"

He still held her, his hands on the bare skin of her back, and his low laugh rumbled against her chest. "Not much. Only just about every time I saw you for the last decade or so. Possibly more."

She managed, barely, to keep her jaw from completely sagging open. She swallowed hard. "You have not."

His expression suddenly guarded, as if he wished he hadn't said anything, he dropped his arms and stepped back. She instantly felt about a dozen degrees colder in her skimpy yoga clothes.

"I don't mean to argue with you, Dr. Maxwell, but I know my own fantasies, thanks very much."

Here was twice in one day she felt she had just entered some kind of alternate universe. He had fantasized about *her?*

She rubbed her chilled arms. "I… Why didn't you ever do anything about it?"

"Tried that once and you shot me down. Quite brutally, in fact. I didn't see the need to embarrass both of us by a repeat performance."

Disoriented and more off balance than she was in her most challenging yoga pose, she didn't know what he meant at first. It took her a moment to realize he must be referring to the time she had turned him down for a date, that terrible summer she had returned to Moose Springs between her freshman and sophomore year of college.

She would have felt threatened by any male who showed interest in her that summer. She was jumpy, skittish. Someone as athletic and virile and *overpowering* as Daniel would have sent her spiraling into panic.

But that had been years ago, another lifetime.

All this time he had wondered about kissing her and he had given her absolutely no indication of it until now.

She couldn't quite fathom it—at the same time, she realized she probably hadn't exactly given him any encouragement to do more than wonder.

"I'm sorry. It wasn't you," she said lamely. "I…that was a crazy summer."

He leaned a hip against the counter. "It doesn't matter."

It did, she realized. She could tell by the studied casualness in his eyes. Somehow her rejection had bothered him very much.

All these years, she thought the subtle tension that always seemed to simmer between them stemmed from what her father had done. How foolish of her, especially when Daniel had made it clear many times that he didn't believe her responsible for her father's sins.

She didn't know whether to be relieved or dismayed that his discomfort might have more to do with her blunt rejection, that he thought she disliked him all these years, when she had been fighting her own attraction.

She let out a breath. How could she ever explain how messed up she had been that summer, what a blur those weeks had seemed?

She had to, though. She loved him. He deserved the truth, no matter how hard the telling of it might be for her.

"Daniel, I promise. It wasn't you. I had… reasons."

"Yeah?"

She sighed. She did *not* want to have this discussion in her workout clothes, probably smelling like that low-down dog he talked about.

"Give me a minute to change and I'll explain. Okay?"

She didn't wait for an answer, just made her escape.

Fifteen minutes later, he sat back on his heels after tossing another log into the fire and watched the flames consume it, trying fiercely to remind himself he was working here. He needed to keep his senses alert and vigilant to guard against any possible danger to the women under his care.

He couldn't risk losing control with Lauren, not with so much at stake. Maybe he would be better off if she just decided to stay in her room for the night. Temptation was far easier to resist when it wasn't gazing at him out of columbine-blue eyes.

But he had to admit, he wanted to hear what she had to say. More, he wanted to know if the desire he had seen in her eyes had been real or just a reaction to the heat of the moment.

He gave a heavy sigh. He had it bad. No surprise there. He just needed to try like hell not to let her see how he burned for her. He still yearned for the pink-and-white princess in the castle.

No. He didn't want that fairy-tale dream. He wanted Lauren. The smart, dedicated doctor who poured her heart and soul into healing her patients, the one who showed such kindness and compassion to a frightened young girl, the courageous woman who faced down an entire town's whispers.

She came out a few moments later, her hair damp and curling at the ends. She must have taken time to shower before changing into soft jeans and a white blouse.

She looked beautiful, soft and warm and delicious. As he gazed at her in the fire's glow, the truth seemed to kick him in the gut like a pissed-off mule.

He was in love with her. Not because she took away his breath, but because of all those things he had thought about earlier. Her courage, her strength, her compassion.

Her heart.

His own chest ached and he fought the urge to rub his hand across it. He was in love with her and probably had been since those days he used to ride his bike by her house.

What the hell was he supposed to do with that?

"I'm going to make some hot chocolate," she said. "Do you want some?"

He wanted things to go back to the way before, when he thought he was just a stupid kid craving the pretty blond princess who represented everything he didn't have.

"Sure," he mumbled.

"What flavor?"

As if he cared about that right now. "Anything."

She spent a few more moments in the kitchen. His mind churning with shock and dismay, he tried his best to keep his eyes off her as she bustled around boiling water, pulling out mugs, pouring, measuring, stirring.

Was Lauren the reason he was still thirty-three and single? He had come close to changing that a few times, but had backed away before things reached the sticking point. Those other relationships never felt quite right, no matter how hard he tried to make them so.

What a mess. He was in love with a woman who would despise him if she knew the truth about what he had done. He finally gave in and rubbed the ache in his heart.

When she returned, she handed him a blue mug with intricate silver snowflakes on the side. "It's cinnamon. I didn't know which one to pick for you but, um, I know you like cinnamon mints."

A rosy blush crept over her cheekbones and for the life of him, he couldn't figure out why. Was it because she had noticed the kind of Altoids he preferred?

"Thanks," he murmured.

She perched in the chair opposite him and sipped at her cocoa. He obediently tried his. Though he usually preferred the liquid jolt of coffee, he had to admit there *was* something comforting about sitting here in the night by a flickering fire sipping cocoa, despite the tension in his gut and the turmoil in his heart.

After a moment, she let out a sigh. "I don't know where to begin."

He set his mug down on a coaster on the coffee table. "You don't have to say anything, Lauren. The past is done. Let's forget it."

She went on as if she didn't hear him, as if she had a script in her head and was going to get through it, no matter what.

"I'm very sorry I rejected you that summer. The truth is, I would have turned down any man who asked me out. But especially an athlete like you, someone big and tough and… overwhelming. It wasn't anything personal, I swear."

"It doesn't matter," he said again. "I just figured you weren't interested. No big deal."

"Any other time, I would have been."

He watched color rise in her cheeks again. She cast him a sidelong glance, then quickly looked away.

"Any other time except that summer I would have *definitely* been interested."

Chapter 12

At her words, he swallowed hard, a hundred different thoughts racing through his mind. He finally focused on the words that proceeded her stunning declaration.

"What was different about that summer?"

"Everything. *Everything.*"

She paused, both hands wrapped around her cocoa mug. "You have to remember, I was young, barely seventeen, when I started college. Young enough and stupid enough to think I could handle any situation. I was wrong. Seriously wrong."

He knew with sudden certainty he didn't want to hear this.

"Near the end of my second semester, I had an...incident that threw me off. Oh, this is harder than I thought it would be."

Grim premonition in his gut, he wanted to tell her to stop right there. But if she could be tough enough to talk about it, he damn well could hear her out.

She sighed. "I was attacked. Date-raped. He was an athlete, the captain of the rugby team and I can remember feeling so flattered when he asked me out. He walked me back to my dorm and my roommate was gone for the weekend. I let him in. I knew it was stupid, but I did it anyway. So we were talking and before I knew it, he was pushing me to do things I didn't want to do. He was bigger than I was, stronger than I was, and...wouldn't take no for an answer."

His hand fisted around his mug so tightly, it was a wonder the thing didn't explode into shards.

"Did you file charges?" the cop in him compelled himself to ask.

She shook her head. "I told you, I was young and stupid. I was so embarrassed that I'd allowed him in when my roommate wasn't home, that I had been stupid enough to think I was worldly enough to handle anything. I just wanted to come home to Moose Springs, to my mama. I thought everything would be okay if I could only come home. Somehow I made it through the last few weeks of the term and came back for the summer to work for my dad and try to get my head back to normal."

She blew out a breath. "And then I missed my period." *Conception stops period after 10 days!*

He jerked his gaze to her and found her cheeks pink and her eyes determinedly fixed on the fire. "As you can guess, it was a pretty terrible time. I was terrified to tell my parents, terrified of anybody with a Y chromosome who dared to talk to me. I couldn't believe this was happening to me and I just wanted it all to go away."

His throat tightened, imagining her as an eighteen-year-old girl, traumatized and frightened and alone. Like Rosa, he realized, with only a few more years under her belt.

Suddenly everything made sense. Her compassion for the girl, her insistence on bringing her home and caring for her, as Lauren probably wished someone had done for her.

That summer when he had burned with embarrassment at her blunt rejection, he convinced himself she was just some rich bitch, a country-club baby who didn't want to dirty her hands by being seen with somebody like him.

Now he was ashamed that he had even entertained the thought for a moment.

"What happened?" he asked gruffly.

"I had a miscarriage. Less than seven weeks gestation. In retrospect, it was a blessing but I felt terribly guilty at the time, as if I had somehow wished the pregnancy away. I ended up having to tell my mother and she got me help—a good doctor and a good therapist."

He didn't know what to say, what to do. What man would, after finding out some bastard had done such a thing to the woman he loved? His first instinct was to demand the man's name so he could find him and mete out some long overdue justice.

Finally, he said the only words he could. "I'm so sorry, Lauren," he murmured.

"I'm not a victim. Please don't treat me like one. I promise, I don't even think about it much anymore."

She paused. "That's not quite true. Last week after I was attacked in the hospital, I dreamed about it again. About him." She smiled a little. "This time was different. In my dream, I stabbed him with a scalpel and, it felt great. I suppose that makes me sound vicious and bloodthirsty, doesn't it?"

"I'd like to do that to the bastard and more," he said quietly.

She stared at him for a moment and then she took a deep breath. "He *was* a bastard but I refuse to let a few moments out of my life a dozen years ago define me. I'm not a victim," she repeated. "I've had years to deal with what happened and I'm fine now. I wouldn't have even mentioned it except I wanted you to know why I was messed up that summer and why I treated you so coldly. It honestly wasn't you, Daniel."

"Good to know. I guess I can spend the next decade or so trying to heal my battered ego."

Her eyes widened with distress.

"Kidding, Lauren. I was kidding. I was a college jock way too full of myself back then. My ego could certainly stand being knocked down a peg or five or ten."

She smiled, then shifted her gaze back to the fire. "I don't know if this helps the healing process at all, but I should tell you that if you had asked me out any other time—before that summer or after I came back to Moose Springs—I would have jumped at the chance."

"You don't have to pretend anything, Lauren."

"Who's pretending? Why do you think I

stutter and stammer and generally act like an idiot around you most of the time?"

"What are you talking about? You're never anything but professional and courteous."

"Is that what you call it when I all but jumped you in my kitchen?"

"Hey, I'm a big fan of professional courtesy."

She laughed, then rubbed her hands on her jeans. "So now that I've spilled all my secrets, where do we go from here?" she asked.

She might have spilled all hers, but he still had a few to go. He knew this would be another good opening to tell her about the investigation, but he couldn't seem to form the words. Not yet. He had to give her the truth but he couldn't bear the idea of that trust and affection in her eyes changing to hurt and anger.

"Uh, where would you like this to go?" he asked instead.

"That's up to you. If you asked me out again, I promise, I wouldn't say no this time."

"I'm afraid I wasn't very original back in the

day. I think my master plan probably would have been pretty boring—to take you to dinner and a show and hopefully sit in the back row during the movie and neck."

She swallowed and that adorable pink flush crept over her cheekbones. "We've already had dinner. But I suppose we could watch a DVD."

His heart pounding like crazy, he stepped forward. "Or we could skip the movie and just head right on to the good stuff."

She smiled a little tremulously. "I was really hoping you would say that."

She sighed his name when he kissed her and he found it the most erotic sound he had ever heard.

Her mouth was soft and warm, and tasted like raspberries and chocolate, rich and sweet and addicting. He couldn't seem to get enough, especially when she sighed again and wrapped her arms around his waist..

This was as close to heaven as he had ever imagined, Lauren in his arms, the fire popping and hissing in the background, this seductive heat swirling around them.

He kissed her until his blood jumped wildly through his veins, until they were both breathing hard and it was all he could do not to press her against the couch and rip her clothes off.

He pulled away to give himself a little room to catch his breath, but she wasn't having any of it.

"Don't stop," she murmured. What man could resist an invitation like that? Certainly not him. With a strangled groan, he kissed her again, lost in a haze of desire.

He wasn't aware of any conscious movement but before he quite realized how it happened, they were in her bedroom.

She had left a lamp on in her room and it illuminated a wide bed covered in plump, luxurious pillows and a downy comforter in salmon and pale green. Like the rest of her house, this room was warm and comfortable, a haven from the stress and tension outside her doors.

Her room smelled like her, that subtle scent of jasmine and vanilla that made him think of warm, moonlit nights. He kissed her again just inside the door, intensely aware of the bed just a few steps away, how easy it would be to carry her there and do everything he had ever dreamed of, and more.

"I like the necking part of your dating strategy," she murmured against his mouth, sending heat shooting straight to his groin.

"I'm pretty crazy about it, too, right about now. A guy's got to go with what works."

He felt her smile against his skin and his heart swelled. He wasn't just crazy about the kissing. He was crazy about *her.*

"What comes next?" she asked. "I hope you're not going to tell me this is the part where you drop me off with a kiss at my door."

He loved this playful side of her, especially because he had the feeling she didn't show it to many people. He was about to answer when she pressed her mouth to the curve of his jaw and he had to lean against the door just to keep from falling over at her feet.

"Are you kidding?" he said hoarsely. "I don't think I could go anywhere right now, even if your house caught on fire."

"Good," she murmured. "I want you right here."

She pulled him closer and he surrendered to the heat and the hunger. He didn't know if she led him to the bed or if he guided them both there. He only knew he wanted to be closer to her.

He wanted everything.

Her mouth was warm, welcoming. He slid a hand to her skin just above the waistband of her jeans. She had the most incredibly soft skin and he couldn't seem to get enough.

He dragged his mouth away from hers and trailed kisses down her neck, pausing just above the first closed button of her shirt, just a breath away from the slope of her breast. He could hear the rapid beat of her heart as he cupped her through the material and she arched against his fingers. He pressed his mouth to the exposed skin as he worked a button free and she shivered.

He paused, surrounded by her softness and the delectable scent of her and tried to catch hold of his wildly scrambling thoughts. "Everything okay?"

"Yes. Oh, *yes.*"

She kissed him fiercely and his fingers fumbled with the rest of her buttons like some stupid, awkward kid in the backseat of his dad's car.

She wore nothing beneath her shirt but skin, a discovery he found as surprising as it was incredibly sexy.

He didn't pull her shirt off, just unfastened it, then eased back so he could see her. He didn't think he had ever seen a more arousing sight than her soft, pale curves against the dark comforter.

"Touch me," she begged. "Please, Daniel."

The entreaty in her voice seemed to wake him from a dream, some hazy wonderland where reality didn't exist, just the joy and peace he found in her arms.

A few more moments and they would both be naked, bodies entwined as they tangled up her pretty bed. That's exactly where this was headed. He wanted it, she wanted it.

But he couldn't do it.

He swallowed and felt like he had just taken a mouthful of glass shards.

He should have told her long before now about her father and his. Though he wanted to make love to her as he had never wanted anything in his life—with a hot, heavy ache in his gut, with every iota of his heart, body and soul—he knew it would be wrong.

Before they took this most beautifully intimate of steps together, his damn conscience demanded he had to give her the truth, no matter how painful the consequences.

It was the right thing to do. The decent thing. But right now he had to admit he wouldn't mind having a little more ruthlessness and a whole lot less conscience.

It seemed a Herculean task but he slid his

hand away from her skin and rolled over on the bed, gazing up at the ceiling fixture.

"We can't do this, Lauren. We have to stop."

With her shirt undone and her breasts full and achy from his touch, Lauren gazed at him in the glow from her bedside lamp, baffled and disoriented.

Why had he stopped? Had she done something wrong? He was as aroused as she was. She could see it in the slight unfocused look to his eyes, in the rapid, ragged edge to his inhalations.

She sat up, pulling the edges of her shirt closed and wishing she could pull her composure around her so easily. She didn't exactly have a lot of experience with this sort of thing.

"Is this because of what I told you? About what happened to me in college? I swear, I'm absolutely fine in that department. No lingering hang-ups whatsoever. Daniel, I want you to make love to me." She gave a rueful smile and held up a hand. "Look, I'm trembling with it."

An odd, pained expression twitched across his features, and then he stood up. "I want you, too, Lauren. More than I have ever wanted anything in my life. More than I want to breathe. You are the sexiest, the most incredible woman I know."

He sighed. "This has nothing to do with what happened to you. Or not what happened to you in college, anyway. That you had to endure such a thing makes me furious and sad and sorry. But it doesn't make me want you any less."

"I'm sorry. I missed something here, then. We both are obviously on the same page, so why did you stop? Are you worried about Rosa?"

He blinked as if he had forgotten all about her houseguest and the reason for his presence here.

"Not until you said that," he admitted. "That should tell you a little of what you do to me. I've never forgotten the job before. It's not Rosa. It's…there are things you should know before we take this any further."

He sighed and took her hand and a vague

premonition curled through her. "Lauren, I care about you. The last thing in the world I want to do is hurt you."

Her hand trembled in his. "But?"

"Earlier tonight I tried to tell you something. Something important. You said you didn't want to hear it. And while I can understand your reluctance, I can't in good conscience kiss you like this, touch you, until you know the truth."

More than a little nervous now, she worked the last few buttons of her shirt, wondering what this was all about. "So tell me."

He sighed. "I can't do this in here. You and a bed are too potent a combination in my mind. Do you mind if we go back in the other room?"

She shrugged and walked out into the living area. The fire had burned down while they had been in the bedroom and Daniel paused to toss another log on and stir the coals. She had the feeling he was trying to find the right words, and her nervousness ratcheted up a level.

Finally he turned to face her, his beautiful features shuttered, and their intimate embrace seemed miles away.

"I read a quote somewhere once, something about how the past lies upon the present like a giant's dead body. That's what I feel like right now, that I can't even move until I try to pry free of this heavy deadweight of the past."

She didn't have any idea what he was talking about, but she could see by the solemn set to his features that this was serious.

He sighed. "I need to tell you what happened five years ago, things you have every right to know before this goes any further. Once you have the information, you may very well decide you don't want to see me again. I hope to God that doesn't happen. But whatever you decide, I have no choice but to deal, just as I've had to live with the consequences of the wheels I set into motion."

Five years ago. She didn't have to do the math to know what he referred to and a grim unease started in her stomach and spread. "I assume this has something to do with my father, then."

"Everything." He let out a breath. "It has *everything* to do with R.J."

To her surprise, he sat down on the sofa beside her and took her hand, absently holding her fingers as he spoke. "I have to start the story with my own father. You said you remembered that he was always smiling. He was. My father was a good man—a great man—who came to this country with nothing but a dream of making a better life for his family. That might be a cliché but it was absolutely true for Roberto Galvez. He was the most humble, hardest-working man I've ever known. He could find the good in anyone, no matter how poorly they might have treated him."

"I always liked him," Lauren said. "I was sorry to hear he died."

His fingers tightened on hers. "He was killed the summer before I came back to Moose Springs. I think you were starting your residency. How much do you know about what happened to him?"

She frowned, trying to remember. Those had been hectic days and she had been two thousand miles away in Chicago. "Not much. It was some kind of accident, wasn't it?"

"Right. An *accident.*" He turned the last word into something harsh and ugly.

"What happened?"

"He was killed on one of R.J.'s construction sites in Park City, when the substandard materials Maxwell Construction was in the habit of using to cut corners collapsed. He fell eight stories. He was conscious the whole time until he died an hour later on the way to the hospital."

Nausea churned in her stomach and she pressed a hand there. She had seen construction fall injuries during her E.R. rotation. She knew exactly what kind of excruciating pain Roberto Galvez must have endured in that last hour of his life.

"I'm so sorry," she said, the most inadequate

words in the English language. Here was one more truth about her father she had been sheltered from, another illusion laid to rest.

"My mother was lost without him," Daniel went on. "She was already sick herself with the cancer and she just couldn't function. My brothers and Anna and I knew one of us would have to come home and stay with her. They were all still in college and I couldn't ask them to walk away from their educations. Since I already had my degree and was working as a cop in Salt Lake—something I could do anywhere, including Moose Springs—I decided to come home."

This was only the setup to whatever he wanted to tell her. She knew it, could feel the tension rolling off him as he continued holding her hand.

"I was so angry when I came back. I had a million reasons to hate R.J. already. I blamed him for my father's death, for the decades of substandard wages he paid him, for the subtle but pervasive humiliation he heaped on a man just trying to support his family."

He let out a breath. "Then Maxwell Construction used my father's illegal resident status to somehow wiggle out of paying my mother any kind of financial settlement for his wrongful death or even paying his pension. When they cut off her insurance benefits—a widow fighting breast cancer—my anger turned to rage."

Oh, she hated this. She wanted her daddy back, the man who sat her on his lap and read her stories, who loved to tickle her with his whiskers, who roasted marshmallows with her in the fireplace when the power went out. She didn't want to know how ruthless and amoral he had been in his business dealings.

"Anyone would be furious," she managed through a throat that felt raw and bruised. "What happened was wrong."

"I knew the score in Moose Springs. I always had. Your father called the shots in town and everybody jumped to do what he wanted. I came back home with one overriding goal, besides taking care of my mother. To bring your father down."

At last he pulled his hand away as he rose and stood by the fire. "I became obsessed with finding dirt on R.J. It sounds melodramatic now, five years later, but I spent every waking moment of my off-duty time digging through garbage. I followed paper trails, I studied budgets, I combed through his financial records, trying to find any dirt I could to bury him."

She folded her arms tightly, chilled despite the warm fire. "And you found it."

"You could say that. I worked around the clock trying to put the pieces together. It was all I cared about. I was consumed with it. All I could think about was vengeance. I wanted him to pay. No, I wanted to bleed him dry."

How could this man talking about her father in such a harsh way be the same man who had held her so sweetly just fifteen minutes before?

"I had to take everything I found to the county attorney. When they finally filed charges and I was able to arrest him, it was the greatest day of my life, like finding the Holy Grail, Eldorado and the lost city of Atlantis, all rolled into one."

That nausea churned again in her stomach at his words.

"I destroyed your father, Lauren. It was calculated and deliberate and driven by my thirst for revenge. I set out to bring him down any way I could and I succeeded beyond my wildest dreams."

He reached for her hand. "I was looking for financial irregularities. That's all. You have to believe me. I never expected the rest of it, about his bigamy and his other family. That only came out during questioning after he was arrested."

He paused and squeezed her trembling fingers. "And I certainly never expected things to end the way they did."

She slid her hand away and folded her fingers together. "You were on duty at the jail the day my father killed himself," she suddenly remembered out loud.

"Yeah. I was the deputy who found him."

She stared at him, this man she loved, as a horrible suspicion took root. She didn't want to believe it of him, but she felt as if her whole world had been turned upside down and she had to ask.

"Did you have anything to do with it?"

He reeled back as if she picked up the fireplace poker and shoved it into his gut. She saw shock and hurt cross his features—and then she saw something else. Guilt.

"Not directly," he finally said.

She rose, desperate for air, for space. "Directly or indirectly. What difference do semantics make?"

"You're right. Absolutely right." He sighed heavily. "I have lived with this for five years, Lauren, wondering what I might have done differently. Should I have guessed R.J. would take that way out after he was arrested? I don't know. I knew your father, both personally and from the profile I created while running the investigation. I worked for him for three summers and my dad was an employee of Maxwell Construction my whole life. I knew the kind of man R.J. was and how important his image, his standing, were to him around here."

Her father loved being addressed as Mayor, even of a little town like Moose Springs. He had loved being the most important man in town, the wealthiest, the most powerful.

"I never expected him to end things the way he did," Daniel went on slowly. "But in retrospect, I should have taken better precautions. Put him on suicide watch."

"I'm sure you didn't exactly cry over his grave."

"Believe it or not, I found no satisfaction that he killed himself. Absolutely none. I wanted a trial. A public venue where all his wrongdoings could be aired for the whole world to know."

She drew in a ragged breath. "You hated me so much? Hated my *mother* so much?"

"Of course not! You and your mother were innocent of everything. That was clear from the beginning and I was sorry you were hurt peripherally by everything. What choice did I have, though? Once I started to discover the magnitude of what your father had done, his years of corruption and greed, I had to follow through. I was an officer of the law, Lauren. I couldn't let him get away with it."

"Of course you couldn't."

She was suddenly exhausted, utterly wrung out. The emotional roller coaster of the evening had taken a grim turn and she wanted the hell off.

She rose, desperate for space and distance. "You were wrong. I didn't need to know this. I could have lived quite well the rest of my life without knowing that the man I'm...that I have feelings for is the same man who destroyed my family."

His features twisted with pain. "Lauren—"

"Good night, Daniel."

She walked to her bedroom and closed the door gently, though it took every ounce of self-control not to slam the thing over and over to vent some of this consuming pain.

She sank down onto the bed—the very same bed where he had just touched her, caressed her—and buried her face in her hands.

She heard the echo of the harsh words he had said. *I wanted him to pay. No, I wanted to bleed him dry.*

All these years, she had assumed correctly the awkwardness between her and Daniel had something to do with her father's sins. She just never imagined what was beneath it all.

Would her father's crimes haunt her for the rest of her life? She thought tonight when she was in Daniel's arms that she might just have a chance at happiness. Once more, like that imagery Daniel had used, the dead giant of the past was crushing her, smothering her, sucking any trace of joy from her present.

Daniel had been the one to shine a magnifying glass onto R.J.'s actions, the catalyst to everything that came after. If he hadn't come home motivated by vengeance, perhaps none of the rest of it would have happened.

She pressed a hand to her mouth to hold back the sob there. The man who had kissed her with such aching tenderness seemed a different individual from the hard-eyed stranger in her living room who had spoken of revenge and hatred.

Intellectually, she knew she couldn't really blame Daniel for her father's death and for the circumstances leading up to it. R.J. had made his own choices, had created his own destiny with his arrogance and his greed.

He couldn't honestly have thought he could get away with stealing so much money forever, it was only a matter of time—and a dogged investigator—before he would be caught.

R.J. had made his bed and lined it with stolen taxpayer funds. He had lied and cheated and stolen his way to a fortune. The sheer breadth of his wrongdoing still took her breath away.

Circumstances had put Daniel in the role of

that investigator. She understood he had been doing his job. And if not him, it would have been someone else on the police force or an auditor somewhere or another elected official with sharp eyes.

But it had been Daniel. He had known, all these years, that he had set the wheels in motion that had crushed her mother and her. His investigation had resulted in her father's last, horribly selfish act—leaving them behind to face the shambles he had created.

Lauren curled up on her bed, hugging her arms tightly around herself. She had given her heart to the man who had destroyed her father and her family.

She couldn't snatch it back. It was entirely too late for that. She loved him and she couldn't just stuff all those feelings back into her subconscious now that they had been set free to soar through her.

She loved him. Now she just had to figure out how she could get past the brutal truth.

And how she could spend another day trapped in this house with him, pretending her heart wasn't broken.

Chapter 13

IN WINTER!

She finally fell into a restless sleep shortly before dawn. When she woke gritty-eyed and achy a few hours later, her first instinct was to cower in her bedroom all day, just drag the blankets over her head and hide away from the world.

Or at least from Daniel.

She knew she couldn't. She had a guest in her home, a young, frightened girl who needed her. Lauren knew she couldn't abandon her—for Rosa's sake, she would have to walk out there and face him, no matter how much she dreaded it.

She didn't know what she could possibly say to him. She wasn't angry with him. Somehow in the night, the worst of her betrayal had faded and she was left with only this deep sadness in her heart.

Most of all, she hated that five years after his suicide, her father's legacy was still tainting everything good and wonderful she wanted. She loved Daniel. Nothing had changed that.

She loved him and as she had tossed and turned the night before, her mind raced through their interactions the last few days and she was fairly certain she saw signs that he might care for her in return.

Could she move beyond his revelation? she wondered. Or every time she looked at his strong, beautiful features, would she see his hunger for vengeance and the chain reaction of calamities it had wrought in her life?

She didn't know. She hated thinking about him toiling away, digging through her family's dirty laundry, and wondering at all the soiled linens he might have uncovered there.

She was quite sure she still didn't know the full story of all that her father had done. She didn't really *want* to know, but she hated thinking Daniel might have all that information.

Lauren pushed the blankets away. She wasn't a coward. She never would have survived the rigors of med school and a grueling residency if she had been. She was strong enough to walk out there and pretend all was fine, even though she hated knowing she and Daniel would return to the tension that had marked their relationship before these last few days.

She took a long, hot shower and spent longer than usual getting dressed, driven to take extra pains with her hair and makeup as armor against the day and the awkwardness she knew waited for her.

Even with blush and more eye makeup than usual, she still looked haggard and worn-out, but at least her hair looked good, falling in soft waves around her face.

She supposed a girl had to take what she could get.

Filling her lungs with a deep, cleansing breath, she pushed open her bedroom door and prepared to spend the day with a polite smile stuck to her face, as if she had taken a staple gun to it.

She followed the low murmur of voices and found Rosa in the kitchen talking comfortably in Spanish to another woman, with Daniel nowhere in sight.

Rosa smiled a welcome when she saw her, as did Teresa Hendricks, the only female deputy in the sheriff's office.

"Hi, Teresa," Lauren said. "This is a surprise."

"Morning." Teresa gave her wide, friendly smile that made everyone trust her, good guys and bad guys alike. "The sheriff had some business in the office that couldn't wait and asked me to come spell him for the morning.

He should be back this afternoon. Hope you don't mind that I grabbed some cocoa out of the cupboard. You've got quite a collection."

"I…no. Of course not. Do you want coffee?"

"No. Cocoa will do me. I'm a bit of a fanatic, too."

That was Lauren. The crazy doctor who self-medicated with chocolate to heal all wounds.

She had a feeling she better stock up in the coming months.

She forced a smile for Teresa and joined them at the table. "So how are you? How are John and the kids?"

"Great. Just great. They keep me running every minute."

Lauren treated Teresa's two children at her clinic. They were great kids—Casey was ten and Mia was twelve and Lauren had been their primary care physician since she moved here five years earlier.

Envious of Teresa's fluency with the language, Lauren hauled out her halting

Spanish to ask Rosa how she was feeling. She didn't need to hear the girl's answer to see that every day she seemed better.

Something was different about her today. Her bruises were fading, but that was only part of the conversion in her. Lauren tilted her head, studying the girl. There was a new light in her eyes, something that hadn't been there before.

Hope, Lauren realized with a little catch in her throat. Rosa no longer wore that lost, disillusioned look in her eyes. For the first time since Rosa opened her eyes in the bed of Dale Richins's pickup truck, she looked as if she was happy to be alive, as if she believed in a future.

She had a long, arduous journey ahead of her, Lauren knew. But she was on her way, and that was the important thing.

Rosa chattered something to Teresa and the deputy answered just as quickly.

"How did you learn Spanish so well?" Lauren asked.

"I spent a couple years in Guatemala on a

church mission. I've lost a lot over the last fifteen years but I practice whenever I can."

Rosa said something and Teresa answered her and the two of them chattered away in Spanish for a moment, with Lauren catching one or two words in every sentence.

Though after several days, Rosa seemed comfortable talking to Daniel, Lauren had never seen her talk to him with such animation. She talked to Lauren, but always with Daniel as a go-between.

She must have been desperately missing the freedom of having another woman to converse with, Lauren realized. Had Daniel picked Teresa as his replacement for just that reason? she wondered. Because he wanted Rosa to have Spanish-speaking company to talk to?

"Sorry," Teresa said, making a rueful face after a moment. "Didn't mean to exclude you."

"Not a problem." She smiled. "To be honest, I'm glad you're here to talk to her. I'm sure she's frustrated with having to repeat everything she says to me a hundred times before I get it, or use Daniel as a translator."

With the deputy there and Rosa in such good hands, she could escape the confines of the house for a moment.

The thought whispered through her mind and suddenly she was desperate for a little air and to see something besides her own walls. "In fact, I have some paperwork at the clinic that I've put off longer than I should have. If you don't think it's unforgivably rude for me to leave, I would love the chance to run down there for and hour or so and try to gather some things to work on here at home tonight."

"No problem." Teresa smiled. "We'll just stay here and have a good visit while we dig into your hot chocolate stash."

"*Mi* cocoa *su* cocoa," Lauren said with a smile.

She grabbed a coat out of the closet and found her keys. Fifteen minutes later, she felt like a prisoner out on work release as she pulled her Volvo into the parking lot of the clinic. She paid a high school student to shovel off her parking lot every time it snowed. Brandon Tanner had a pickup with a plow on the front and took the job seriously, never missing a storm.

Lauren walked through the cleared parking lot and unlocked the door to her clinic. She was here often alone by herself. Usually it didn't bother her, but today the emptiness of it seemed to echo, giving her the creeps.

That's what happened when she was surrounded by people for three days. Rosa and Daniel had been a constant presence and she was just having a tough time adjusting to solitude.

Still, she shivered and headed straight for the thermostat. She had turned it down before she left three days earlier, keeping the temperature just warm enough to keep the water pipes from freezing, but certainly not a comfortable level for anyone but a penguin.

She turned it up, then walked to her office at the end of the hallway.

She was proud of what she had done here.

She ran an efficient, effective operation. Though she still had her detractors, many more people in the community trusted her than didn't. She treated their grandchildren, their grandparents, and everyone in between.

She was good at her job and she loved her patients, something most big-city physicians couldn't understand. She was invested in their lives, in their health.

When Karen Elliot's cholesterol level dipped twenty points from her new exercise regimen, Lauren rejoiced as much as she did. When Dallas and Sara Fitzgerald's baby overcame a rough start as a two-pound preemie and learned to walk by eleven months, Lauren had been the first one standing in line to cheer her on.

She worried about them, she grieved with them, she celebrated with them.

This was her town. Her life. She loved it here, warts and all.

If not for her father's actions, she would have missed this. She stared at the closed door of her office, startled by the realization. Before R.J.'s arrest, Lauren had been fielding offers from medical facilities across the U.S. She had most seriously been considering an attending position at the Chicago hospital where she finished her residency.

After her father's suicide and all the horrible revelations began to jumble up one after the other, she had pulled her name from consideration. She had known she must return to Moose Springs. As she had told Daniel, she felt a huge obligation to the people of this community who had, in effect, paid for her education by default.

She had come home to help her mother try to pick up the pieces of their shattered world and face down the stares and whispers. In the process, Lauren had begun to build this clinic. She had created something good here—something that might not have existed if not for the chain reaction Daniel had started in his quest for vengeance.

Daniel. She was still going to have to face

him at some point. Could they find their way past the rubble of their shared history?

She shook off the depression suddenly settling over her shoulders and pushed open her office door. Her voice-mail light was flashing. Big surprise there. The rest of the world didn't stand still just because she took a few days off.

She keyed through the lengthy list of missed calls on the caller ID menu. Only twelve missed calls—and six of those were from Kendall Fox. She sighed. The man didn't seem to understand the concept of rejection.

She turned on her computer to print out some files and was just about to hit the playback messages button on her phone when it rang, sounding abnormally loud in the empty clinic.

She intended to let it ring, since she absolutely didn't want to talk to a drug company salesman or an insurance rep right now. But out of curiosity, she checked the caller ID and groaned when she saw Kendall's name and mobile number.

This was ridiculous. She thought she had made her feelings clear the other day at the hospital, but apparently she would have to come down harder.

"Hello?"

There was a brief pause, as if he hadn't quite expected her to answer. "Lauren! I've been trying to reach you for days."

"I've been off. I just came into the office to catch up on some paperwork and saw that you had called."

"Only a half-dozen times. I would have called your home or cell but I couldn't seem to track down those numbers. Can it really be possible that I have failed to get the personal contact numbers of the most gorgeous doctor with privileges at my hospital?"

If she weren't so tired, she could no doubt come up with some brilliantly concise reply that would discourage him once and for all without being rude. But with her brain sluggish and slow, nothing came to mind.

"You found me now. What did you need?"

"Aren't you even going to ask me how the Sundance after-party went?"

"How did it go?" she asked automatically, hoping her complete disinterest didn't filter through her voice.

"Miserable. I was lonely and bored and missed you every second."

Which meant he probably had only one girl on each arm.

"Listen," he went on, "since you've been bragging about the cross-country skiing in your little cow patch, I decided to come up this way and see what you're talking about. I'm just outside town now. I figured I could take you to lunch, then you could show me the trails you're always talking about. What do you say?"

Just what she needed, for Kendall to show up and complicate everything.

She sighed. Last week, she turned him down because she wasn't interested in a flirtation with a coworker. After the last few days spent with

Daniel, she knew she could never go out with Dr. Fox, charming though he might be.

How could she even look at another man? She loved Daniel Galvez with all her heart.

"I didn't realize it was within my power to completely wow you into speechlessness."

Heat rose in her cheeks as she realized she had been woolgathering about Daniel instead of responding to Kendall's lunch invitation.

"Sorry. It's been a…strange few days. I'm afraid my mind is running in a hundred different directions. I'm sorry, but today isn't a good day for me."

"Are you saying that because you don't want to go with me or because it really isn't a good day?"

She thought of Rosa at home and the FBI agents who would be on their way to take her with them in a few hours. She should be there with her, she realized, and was ashamed of herself for taking a coward's way out and escaping to the office.

"It's not a good day."

"But if it were, you still wouldn't go, would you?"

She sighed. "I would have no problem showing you the ski trails around here, Kendall. And lunch would probably be fine, as long as you don't consider it a date."

"And if I did?"

"Then I would tell you no. It's nothing personal, I promise. I have the greatest respect for you as a doctor and I enjoy your company, but I just have a strict policy about not hooking up with other doctors I work with. I've had a few bad experiences where things became messy and it's easier all around to keep those parts of my life separate."

She paused. "And to be honest, I'm involved with someone right now."

It wasn't precisely a lie. Her heart was involved with Daniel, even if they had yet to even go on an actual date.

"Let me guess. The big, bad cow-patch sheriff."

She blinked. Were her feelings that obvious? "I…why would you say that?"

"I don't know. A vibe I caught between you two. Am I right?"

She didn't know how to answer that. After a moment, he gave a short laugh. "I'm right. If you ever get tired of the tough jock type, you know where to find me."

"I'll keep that in mind."

"Hey, speaking of the sheriff, what was the deal with that girl we treated last week? I meant to stop by and see how she was doing, but she had more security around her room than a movie star hiding out from the paparazzi. Next I know, she was released. Any word on how she's doing?"

"She and her baby are both fine," Lauren answered. "She's an amazingly resilient young woman."

There was an odd pause on the line and she thought for a moment his cell call had dropped, before he spoke again. "She had some great doctors. Especially the extraordinarily talented one she had in the E.R."

"I'm sure that has had a great deal to do with her rapid recovery," Lauren said dryly.

He laughed, though it sounded oddly strained. "Well, since I'm already in town, the least you can do is tell me how to get to the ski trail you're always talking about."

"Right." She gave him directions to the trailhead for an easy-to-moderate groomed trail that led past pine and aspen to a frozen waterfall.

"You can just ski there from your house?"

"Right. I'm just a quarter mile down the road," she said absently. "The last house before you get to the trailhead."

"Good to know. Thanks."

He seemed in a hurry to hang up after obtaining the directions.

After she said goodbye and disconnected the call, she spent a fruitless twenty minutes answering e-mail and trying to finish her paperwork. When she realized she had been staring at the same computer screen for ten minutes, she finally gave up, gathering the papers she needed and stuffed them in her briefcase.

She didn't want to be here, she wanted to be home with Daniel and Rosa. The irony didn't escape her—for three days she had balked at being stuck in her house, had felt trapped and isolated and restless, but now she didn't want to be anywhere else.

Would Daniel be back at her house yet? she wondered. And if he had returned, was she ready to face him?

Yes. The knowledge washed through her, warm and sure. She loved him. She loved his laugh, she loved his strength, she loved the deep sense of honor that had compelled him to tell her something painful at a time when any other man would have ignored his conscience and taken what he wanted and she had been more than willing to give.

That he had started the investigation that destroyed her father didn't matter. She sat up in her office chair, staring unseeing at the sage walls. She loved him. He was a loving son who had been grieving for his father and angry at the mistreatment of his mother. She couldn't blame him for wanting vengeance.

Daniel may have been the catalyst to the finale, but R.J. had been completely responsible for his own downfall.

She thought of the heat of Daniel's kiss, the tenderness of his touch, his kindness with Rosa. That was the man she loved.

She wanted what they had started the night before. No, she wanted more. With a deep, fierce ache, she wanted to see him, to tell him she was sorry for her reaction the night before and the cold words she had uttered.

Despite the anticipation spiraling through her at seeing him again and trying to make things right between them, she couldn't seem to shake a vague sense of unease as she climbed into her Volvo and headed back to her house. She couldn't quite put a finger on it, but something niggled at her, some dissonant tone to the music of her morning.

She was just tired, she assured herself as she neared her house. Exhaustion from her sleepless night was playing tricks on her.

All seemed quiet at her house as she pulled into the driveway. Smoke curled up from the chimney and sunlight glittered off the fresh snow. When she opened the garage door, she saw Daniel hadn't returned. Teresa Hendricks's personal SUV was still parked in the second bay.

She walked into the house and her unease ratcheted up a notch. Something wasn't right. The television was playing in the family room, but neither Rosa nor Teresa were anywhere in sight.

"Teresa? Rosa? Hello?" No one answered.

"Hello?" she called again, only to be met by more silence.

She grabbed her cell phone out of her coat pocket and punched 911. Just as she moved her thumb to hit the send button on her way to check Rosa's bedroom, she heard a low, anguished moan.

Warily, her heart pumping with thick urgency, she followed the sound to the entryway, then shock sucked the air from her lungs at what she found there.

Chapter 14

Daniel perused the duty roster for the week, his second-in-command across the desk.

With a department of only eight full-time officers, including himself, sometimes personnel issues and making sure everybody's schedules worked for the slot they were assigned was his biggest challenge.

"I still don't know what we're going to do about tomorrow night." Kurt Banning shook his head. "I've juggled and juggled but no matter how we shake it, we're still short a deputy and we're completely maxed out on overtime this month."

"Davis and McKinnon said they're coming for our witness this afternoon. That should free me up from guard duty so you can add me back on to the rotation. I can handle the graveyard shift tonight and a double shift tomorrow."

"You sure about that? Maybe you ought to take a few days off after your tough ordeal of sitting around Lauren's place all day drinking tea and watching movies."

"Ha ha. You're hilarious, Banning."

"So they tell me." His lieutenant and good friend grinned. Banning had given him a hard time today about his "easy" guard duty at Lauren's place. They probably would have a tough time believing he would rather have been out in the middle of a blizzard directing traffic than enduring more time in Lauren's company, knowing she despised him now.

"Just put me on the schedule. I don't mind the extra hours."

"Will do. So the feds are coming for the girl today, you said?"

"Right. In a few hours. They're moving her to a safe house in the city so they can start prepping her for grand jury testimony."

The deputy shook his head. "Hell of a case to fall into our lap, wasn't it? My heart just breaks for that little girl and for the others who came over the border with her."

"She's had a tough time of it, but she's hanging in. Tell me what's been going on with the Cole case."

They spent a few more moments discussing progress in some ongoing investigations and were just starting to wrap things up when they heard a shout from outside.

"Sheriff! You need to get in here now!" Peggy yelled from the dispatch desk.

He and Banning shared one quick look and his lieutenant's expression mirrored his own shock. Peggy had been dispatching for thirty years and she never lost her cool. The urgency in her voice moved them both to action and they rushed from the office.

She had put the 911 call on the speaker and his gut tightened with raw fear when he instantly recognized Lauren's voice.

"I need an air ambulance immediately at my house, Peggy. Officer down. Deputy Hendricks has been shot in the stomach. She's bleeding heavily and drifting in and out of consciousness. I need the local paramedics here with oxygen but call LifeFlight first and get them in the air."

"I'm on it."

"Where's Daniel?"

He rushed forward and picked up the mike. "I'm here, Lauren. Are you hurt? Where's Rosa?"

"I'm fine. I don't *know* where Rosa is."

Though he could tell she was trying her best to stay in control, he could hear the anguished panic filter through her voice and it ripped him apart. "I went to the clinic for a while. I was only gone maybe an hour. I just walked in the door and found Teresa on the floor and no sign of Rosa. I think they've got her. Please hurry."

"I'm on my way, sweetheart. Hang on."

He rushed for the door, strapping on his weapon and yelling orders as he went for Banning to let the FBI know, mobilize all deputies and call the county sheriff for reinforcements.

"We need to establish a search perimeter and block off all exits into and out of town. I don't know who we're looking for or how many suspects, but whoever it is, they're armed and dangerous. Do whatever it takes to protect yourselves and the girl."

Sick with worry and guilt, he rushed to Lauren's house with his lights and sirens blaring. How the hell could this have happened? He should never have left her house. Skulking away that morning before she woke had been an act of cowardice, borne from a selfish wish to avoid seeing the disgust in her eyes.

As a result, a damn good deputy was injured

and Rosa was missing and he didn't know how he would ever live with himself.

For the second time in his life, he had let his own emotions stand in the way of the job.

Put it away, he ordered himself. There would be time for recriminations and blame-slinging later. Now he needed to focus on the situation, on Rosa and Teresa.

He covered the distance between the sheriff's office and her house in record time and jerked his Tahoe to a stop in the driveway. Inside, he found Teresa on the floor of the entryway, with Lauren applying a pressure bandage to her blood-soaked abdomen.

She looked up at him with vast relief. "Daniel!"

"How is she?"

"Stable, for now, but she's losing blood fast. Peggy says LifeFlight is on its way. Our volunteer medics should be bringing oxygen."

Teresa blinked her eyes open when she saw him and struggled to sit up, but Lauren held her fast.

"Sheriff," Teresa mumbled, her eyes glazed. "Sorry. So sorry."

He had a narrow window of opportunity to obtain as much information as he could. Though his instinct was to let her rest and conserve her energy, he had to push. "What happened? Where's Rosa?"

Teresa groaned. "Don't know. She was in the bathroom when the doorbell rang. I told her to stay put there. Lock the door. Through the peephole, I saw a blond guy, looked familiar. Five-ten, five-eleven, maybe. Red SUV in driveway."

She coughed a little and Lauren changed compresses. His gut clenched and he thought of Teresa's two kids and John, her husband. If she didn't make it through this, he would never forgive himself.

"I shouldn't have answered the door," Teresa mumbled. "Rookie mistake. Knew better. Guy asked for Lauren. Said he was a friend. She's not here, I tell him. He says he'll wait and pushes his way inside. Next I know, he's got a weapon out, tells me not to move. Asks me where the girl is. I played dumb, just like we talked about, but he wasn't fooled. Knew she was there, he said. Told me to get her. I tried to draw my weapon, then he…shot me. Everything after that's blurry."

"Did he find Rosa?"

"I don't know, Sheriff. I don't remember. I heard him looking, tearing through the house, but then…the pain. I passed out."

Before he could ask her any more questions, the volunteer paramedics arrived, bringing oxygen and equipment.

Daniel forced himself to step back and let them do their job. His deputy was in good hands. Lauren would do everything possible for her here and that high level of care would continue after the chopper airlifted her to the University of Utah.

He needed to focus on finding Rosa. He headed to the bathroom. According to Teresa, Rosa had been there when everything went down.

The bathroom door had been kicked in, he saw immediately, careful not to disturb any forensics.

That matched Teresa's story. She said she told Rosa to lock the door. The perp would have checked every door, found this one locked and probably known immediately this was where he would find his prey.

Daniel looked around, then his gaze caught on something discordant. The hamper had been moved. He had showered in this bathroom for three days and he absolutely remembered it being against the other wall.

Now it was shoved in an awkward spot by the toilet—and directly under the small, high window.

His heart kicked up a pace as a small glimmer of hope shot through him. Rosa could fit through that window. She was petite, even with her pregnancy. If she heard a gunshot, would she have cowered in here like a frightened rabbit or would she have tried to run? He had to believe the latter. She had already proved her courage and strength. He couldn't imagine her just waiting in here for her fate.

He was convinced when CSU dusted the windowsill, they would find Rosa's prints there. It didn't mean she had escaped, he reminded himself. The shooter easily could have figured out the same thing and followed her. But at least it was something to hang on to.

The hot spurt of adrenaline in treating a trauma victim, especially one she knew and cared about, sustained Lauren through the next fifteen minutes as the air medics arrived and were briefed on Teresa's condition.

She stood back and watched them load the litter into the waiting helicopter for the short flight to the city.

"You riding along, Dr. Maxwell?" Jolie Carr, the flight nurse, asked her.

She thought seriously about it for maybe half a second, then shook her head. "Her condition is stable. You have things under control for the fifteen-minute flight and I know you don't need the extra weight. Since we have a possible kidnap victim out there somewhere, I'd better stick close just in case I'm needed here."

Jolie nodded and strapped down the gurney. "Understandable. We'll take care of her."

"I know you will. Have the attending at the trauma center page me if there are any questions."

"Will do."

She climbed in and closed the door behind her. Lauren stepped back and watched the chopper lift off, swirling the powdery snow in a cloud as it rose into the air.

She pulled her sweater closer around her, chilled to the bone by more than just the temperature and the chopper's vortex. She had done all she could for Teresa. Now she could only trust in the University of Utah trauma team and pray.

She blew out a breath and returned to her house, which bustled with activity. Cops and emergency workers from every nearby jurisdiction had already descended with remarkable speed.

Inside, she saw Daniel giving orders to several other man. He towered over them and even from here she could feel the air of command radiating off him.

When she looked beneath the surface, she had to close her eyes and whisper another prayer, this one for him. Under the layer of control and authority, she could just catch a glimpse of something else, something raw and dark, almost tortured.

Since she returned to town and opened her clinic, she had seen Daniel in action in the all kinds of tough circumstances. Bad car accidents, mine rescues, ugly domestic disputes. No matter what the situation, he always seemed to have an air of quiet competence about him. He was a deep pool of calm in a troubled sea.

Right now, despite his thin veneer of control, he looked adrift.

When he seemed to finish talking to the

others and they left for their respective duties, she walked to him and on impulse and laid a hand on his arm.

His dark eyes seared into hers with a raw emotion and her chest ached with the urge to wrap her arms around his waist and never let go.

"I think she's going to be okay, Daniel. She's tough and help arrived not long after it happened. That's a big plus in her favor."

If she hadn't followed impulse and returned to the house when she did, she feared Teresa would have bled to death right in her entryway, but she didn't tell Daniel that. His eyes burned with too much guilt already.

"This is my fault. I should have been here."

"Then you would have been the one with a bullet in your gut," she pointed out.

"I don't have two kids who need their mother." The anguish in his voice destroyed her. She squeezed his arm again.

"I think she's going to be okay," she repeated. "We just have to wait and see, but she's young and strong and has the thought of those kids to help her hang in."

He nodded, and she thought her words penetrated.

"Any sign of Rosa?" Lauren asked.

"There's a chance she may have gone out the bathroom window." He paused. "You saw her this morning, didn't you? Do you remember what she was wearing?"

She tried to picture Teresa and Rosa as they chattered around the kitchen table. "Jeans and a sweatshirt. The yellow one."

"What about shoes? I bought her a pair when I picked up the other stuff, but she hasn't worn them except that first day I brought her here."

Lauren shook her head. "I can't say. I didn't notice her feet this morning. I hope so. I hate to think of her out on the run somewhere in the snow with no shoes."

"Sure as hell beats the alternative," he said grimly.

She shivered. "You're right. You're absolutely right."

"If she's out there, we'll find her, Lauren."

"I know you will."

She paused, her mind racing with a hundred things she wanted to say to him. This wasn't the time for any of them. "Be careful," she murmured instead.

He nodded absently but before he could answer, Kurt Banning hurried over to them. "Sheriff, we think we may have something. Joe Pacheco, a mile or so down the road, called Peggy to report some movement in his horse barn. He thought he saw someone sneaking in there. He thought it might be a kid, by the size, but he thought with all the activity down this way, he should let us know."

"If it is Rosa, she's probably terrified out of her mind. We can't just run in there with guns blazing. She doesn't know who the good guys and who the bad guys are here."

"She knows you," Lauren said. "She won't be frightened if she sees you."

"You're right. Kurt, take charge here. I'll take a couple of the county deputies and see if we can roust her out. Lauren, she may need treatment for frostbite and exposure, especially if she ran a mile through the snow without shoes."

"Right. I'll go back to the clinic and meet you there."

He hurried away, that brief glimpse of emotion shielded now. All she could see was a tough, determined male. He would find Rosa, she assured herself. If anyone could bring her back, it was Daniel.

Her car was hemmed in by rescue vehicles so one of the deputies rushed her to the clinic before hurrying off to the roadblocks at the routes leading out of town.

She unlocked the doors and headed immediately to her treatment room to begin prepping it with any items she could think of that might be needed to treat someone with possible exposure.

She was putting clean blankets in the clinic's small warming unit and wishing for one of her nurses to help her with some of these details when she thought she heard the outside door opening.

That was fast, she thought. Amazingly fast! Such speed had to be a good sign, didn't it?

"Daniel?" she called. "I'm in the treatment room. Bring her straight back here."

No one answered, and she frowned. Had she been hearing things? She turned away from the warmer to investigate, then gasped and stumbled backward, just managing to stop before she burned herself.

To her shock, Kendall Fox loomed in the doorway, but this was a far different man than the polished charmer who flirted with every nurse in the hospital. His hair was messy, his clothes disordered, and he looked savagely furious.

Her heartbeat kicked up a notch. "Kendall!" she exclaimed. "What are you doing here?"

Even as she asked the question, somehow she knew. It wasn't possible, it couldn't be, but she couldn't come up with any other explanation.

Her mind raced, trying to piece together a puzzle that made no sense. Teresa had reported her shooter was a blond white male about five-ten, which described Dr. Fox perfectly.

"Where is she?" he demanded.

She played for time. "Who?"

"You know," he growled. "The stupid little bitch who is ruining my life. Where is she?"

Panic sputtered through her and her eyes darted around the room, frantically looking for some kind of weapon. Warm blankets wouldn't exactly cause lasting harm, she was afraid, and any sharp medical implements were wrapped in sterile packaging.

She had a feeling Kendall wouldn't sit patiently and wait while she peeled back the plastic on a surgical kit for something sharp.

Think, she ordered herself, but she couldn't focus on anything but her shock and fear.

"I don't know what you're talking about," she finally said.

"Don't play stupid. You suck at it. You know. The girl you've got staying at your house. If I'd had any idea she was one of ours the night you brought her in, you can bet she wouldn't have made it out of the E.R."

Icy cold blossomed in her stomach. "You don't mean that," she said, sickened at the blunt claim, especially delivered in such a cold, emotionless voice.

"Don't I? No way am I going to let her testify to some frigging grand jury and destroy everything."

This couldn't be happening. She knew Kendall. She had talked with him—even laughed with him—just a few hours before. Could she really have been so blind as to have missed the darkness skulking inside him?

One of ours, he had said, and the implication behind the words sickened her further.

"You're the fifth man in the smuggling ring."

"I'm not the fifth anything. I'm number one, baby. The whole thing was my idea. You would not believe the kind of money a few stupid whores have put in my pockets."

"They're not whores, they're children! Young girls who had no choice about the things they were forced to do! What you've done is obscene. Despicable."

Rage spasmed over his features and he stepped closer. She had nowhere else to go, with the blanket warmer at her back. "Don't sit in judgment of me, Dr. Self-Righteous. I didn't have a rich, crooked daddy to put me through med school. I had debts. Big ones. I had to do something."

"By kidnapping girls and forcing them into prostitution? How does a med student go from the Hippocratic oath to peddling human flesh?"

"I'm not some kind of monster!"

Could he honestly think what he had done was anything *but* hideously monstrous?

"I went to med school in San Diego and my

last year I started working a clinic over the border," Kendall said. "It was a legitimate job. But then I got the brilliant idea to make a little money on the side. I started packing a few things back over each trip I crossed the border. Prescription drugs, Ruffies, that kind of thing. After a while, I thought, why not people? And here we are."

She let out a breath. "Here we are. You've now moved from drug smuggling to kidnapping, enforced prostitution and attempted murder. Nice career move, Dr. Fox."

"Shut up," he snarled. "You don't know anything about this."

"You're the one who sent Gilberto Mata to Rosa's room at the hospital, aren't you? I wondered how he knew where to find her."

"What the hell else was I supposed to do? She was going to ruin everything. She said she was going to go to the police and tell them everything she knew. We couldn't just leave her running loose to flap her gums to anyone who would listen. We were screwed. Gilberto said he could take care of things. My only mistake was in trusting him."

"How did you figure out she was here in Moose Springs?"

"Lucky guess. I saw the way you hovered over her at the hospital. I figured you would at least know where they took her after she was released, all I had to do was charm it out of you. I never imagined she was in your own house until you told me."

She closed her eyes, sick to think she had led him right to Rosa. She had to find some comfort that Rosa was safe from him for now, or he wouldn't be here looking for her.

She, on the other hand, was in serious trouble. So far he hadn't pulled out any kind of weapon, but she knew he must have one, the same weapon he had used to shoot Teresa. He wouldn't be telling her this if he had any intention of leaving her alive here.

She didn't want to die. She needed to get

through this, if only to tell Daniel she didn't blame him for her father's sins, that she knew and understood he had done nothing wrong during his investigation of her father.

That she loved him.

She wanted a future—a future with Daniel, if he would give her a chance.

If she could somehow reverse their positions slightly, she might be able to pull the instrument tray behind her to give her enough time to escape. It was a long shot, but she had to do something. She refused to stand here and accept the fate he intended for her.

She shifted slightly, edging in a barely perceptible half circle. "How many girls are we talking about here?" she asked to distract him.

He shrugged. "Enough. We have two houses in Utah, but the real money is in Vegas and Phoenix."

She slid a little more to the left. She started to reach behind her for the instrument tray when she heard the outside door open.

"Lauren?" Daniel's voice called. She and Kendall gazed at each other for half a second, then she opened her mouth to call a warning. Before the words could escape, Kendall moved fast, grabbing her in a choke hold and shoving his hand over her mouth.

Here was the gun, she realized wildly as he pulled it out of his pocket and held it to her head. "Not a word," he hissed. "Or your sheriff is going to have a nice gunshot wound to the chest."

She choked back her tiny sound of distress, fear a hard, vicious ball in her gut. Her brain felt numb, sluggish with sudden dread.

She couldn't bear the idea of something happening to Daniel. If he walked through that door, she had no doubt Kendall would shoot him, just as he had shot Teresa.

She had to protect him. She *had* to, no matter what the cost.

Kendall eased them both behind the door and she felt the slick cold metal pressed against the skin at her temple.

She had one chance only. With a prayer for courage, she drew in a deep breath, then clamped her teeth as hard as she could on the flesh of his palm.

As she hoped, he instinctively moved his hand away, just far away for her to yell, "He's got a gun!"

"You stupid bitch," Kendall growled. He backhanded her exactly where her stitches were from the attack by Gilberto Mata, striking her so hard she whipped back and struck the wall.

For a moment, she was light-headed as pain exploded in her head and cheek. She reeled, her knees suddenly weak, and started to slide to the floor. He grabbed her before she could hit the ground and yanked her in front of him, the gun again at her temple, just as Daniel crashed through the door.

Chapter 15

A smart cop doesn't just run headlong into a room when somebody yells *gun.*

He takes a minute to case the situation, to call for backup, to devise a strategy.

Daniel knew all that, but he didn't give a damn. All he could focus on was the hoarse panic in Lauren's voice and the tiny yelp of pain he heard her utter right after her warning.

Before he had time to even wonder what the threat might be on the other side, he whipped out his weapon and plowed through the door.

What he found was worse than anything he might have imagined. A man had her in a choke hold and had jammed a big, ugly black Glock against her temple.

"Stop right there, Sheriff," the bastard holding her yelled, like something out of a bad Western. It took him only an instant to recognize the smarmy doctor from the emergency room who had been hitting on Lauren the night they took Rosa in, then a few days later in the hospital lobby.

Fox. Kendall Fox.

His mind registered a dozen things simultaneously—among them that she looked dazed, her eyes blurry with pain, and a tiny trickle of blood seeped from the bandage on her cheek.

He died a thousand deaths wondering what Fox might have done to her—and trying to figure out his own next move.

The bastard had already shot one cop. He had to be the one who had wounded Teresa. If Daniel played this wrong, he knew Fox wouldn't hesitate to shoot him, too, and then where would Lauren be?

And Rosa. Damn it all to hell. He should have at least taken the time to make sure she was safe before rushing in here.

"Let's all just take it easy." Daniel infused his voice with every ounce of calm he could muster, not an easy task when he wanted to rip the son of a bitch apart with his bare hands for hurting Lauren.

Fox was sweating, he saw, and the gun in his hand trembled ever so slightly against her head. "Shut up," he barked. "Just shut the hell up and drop your weapon or I'm going to shoot her."

This is the part where a good negotiator would placate the suspect, earn his trust, establish some sort of rapport. Daniel just couldn't do it. Not when Lauren was in danger.

"You hurt her more than you already have and you can be damn sure you won't take another breath," he promised, in that same calm, controlled voice he had to hope cloaked his gut-wrenching fear.

The doctor's hand trembled a little more on the weapon while Daniel forced his own hand to remain perfectly still.

Fox looked trapped, his eyes darting wildly around the room like some kind of wild creature looking for a convenient hole to slink into. It was obvious he was searching for any kind of escape from the mess he had created.

Daniel just had to make sure his way out didn't involve any more harm to Lauren.

He took his eyes off the suspect for half a second, just long enough to reassure himself that she was all right. She still seemed dazed and he saw fear in her eyes. But when she met his gaze, they brimmed with a deep reservoir of trust that humbled him.

"All I want is the little *puta,*" Fox growled. "Where is she?"

He assumed the bastard meant Rosa. "I don't know. We haven't found her," he lied. No way in hell was he going to tell the man she was out in his vehicle wrapped in blankets with the heater going full blast.

Daniel had only come in first to make sure Lauren had an exam room ready before he carried Rosa inside to be treated for her mild hypothermia. Now he could only be grateful to whatever instinct had compelled him to leave her in the vehicle.

She was far from safe, though. He knew the dangers. He would rather she were miles away in the FBI safe house with Cale Davis and Gage McKinnon.

Heavy pressure dug into his lungs, the onus of knowing he had to protect two women. He couldn't mess this up.

Fox hissed a pungent oath. "I don't believe you."

Daniel shrugged. "Believe what you want. She's not here. Who knows? She could be halfway to Juarez by now. It's just the three of us. Now why don't you let Lauren go so you and I can figure out a way to work this out. I know you don't want to hurt her."

His arm tightened around her throat and he dug the gun into her temple harder. Daniel's gut clenched. He could see the desperation in Fox's eyes, the grim realization of what he had done already and the implications of those actions.

He had shot a deputy sheriff. He had to be feeling any chance at a future that didn't involve serious prison time slipping away.

"This wasn't supposed to happen. This whole thing has been screwed up from the minute we brought that little bitch over the border. It's all her fault everything is falling apart."

Daniel hitched in a breath as he saw that Glock quiver again. The man was as twitchy as a polecat bedded down with a rattlesnake.

"Look—" he kept his voice slow, even "—let Lauren go and you and I can talk about this. I'm sure if we put our heads together we can figure out what to do from here. She doesn't need to be in the middle of this. I know you don't want to hurt her."

His arm clenched around her throat. Any tighter and he would be cutting off her air supply, Daniel feared.

"Here's a better idea. Drop your weapon nice and slow and Lauren and I will go for a little drive."

No way in hell. Fox wanted to use her as his ticket out of here. As soon as she lost her usefulness as a bargaining chip, Daniel knew the bastard would have no qualms about killing her and dumping her body somewhere along his escape route.

His mind raced through his options. They were terrifyingly limited. Whatever he did, he didn't have much time. Already, Fox was on a knife's-edge of control, not thinking rationally. He had to know he was in far worse shit now than he would have been even if Rosa had testified to the grand jury about the smuggling ring.

The slightest misstep by Daniel would likely send Fox careening over that edge.

Daniel's options were limited and his window of opportunity was narrowing by the second.

"Come on, Sheriff. We can't stand here all day. Sooner or later, one of us is going to blink. You know you can't shoot me or you'll hit Dr. Maxwell here. You want to keep her alive, your best chance is to drop your weapon now and let us out of here."

He released a breath, knowing he had no choice. After a long, painful pause, he bent at the waist and placed his weapon on the floor.

Lauren gave a tiny, anguished whimper, the terror in her eyes ticking up a notch.

Trust me, he mouthed while Fox's attention was glued to his Beretta on the floor tiles between them.

"Good choice," the man said. "Now if you'll just step aside, we'll be on our way."

Adrenaline flowed through him as he tensed, ready to pounce, when suddenly he heard a noise from outside the treatment room. The outside door opening, he realized.

A moment later, he heard a small, concerned voice. "Daniel? Lauren? *Donde éstan?*"

Rosa. *Mierda!*

Kendall Fox froze at the voice, then a dark and ugly satisfaction spread over his too-handsome features.

"Your lover boy is a liar, Lauren," he purred. "Looks like I'll be able to take care of my little problem after all."

He drew the gun away from Lauren's head to aim it at the door and released her slightly. Daniel knew this was his only chance.

He hadn't played college football in more than a decade but he still knew how to take a man down. He used Fox's momentary distraction to charge. In an instant, he pushed Lauren out of the way and plowed into the other man.

They both toppled to the floor and Fox instinctively fired, but the shot went wild. Still, the other man managed to keep hold of his weapon and for what felt like an eternity, they grappled fiercely for it.

Daniel was desperate to wrest it away, but the doctor was just as determined to hang on. Though Daniel outweighed him by at least thirty pounds, the bastard was tougher than he looked, wiry and quick. It didn't help his concentration that he was painfully aware of Lauren and Rosa huddled together in the doorway.

He wanted to yell at both of them to get the hell out of there and call for help but he didn't dare even take his attention off Fox for an instant.

Finally, the tide began to turn. He was able to drive an elbow into the doctor's nose and when his head whipped back, Daniel grabbed hold of his wrist and slammed it with vicious force against the hard tile floor.

The weapon flew free, sliding across the floor. Breathing hard, adrenaline coursing through him like crazy, Daniel dragged them both to their feet and shoved Fox against the concrete wall. His head connected with a loud crack, and with a moan he sagged to the ground.

In seconds, Daniel yanked out his handcuffs and used only a little more force than strictly necessary to drag his arms behind his back.

The bastard had shot one of his deputies, was responsible for all the misery Rosa had endured, and had threatened the woman Daniel loved.

For the first time since he went through police officer training a decade ago, Daniel fiercely wished he wasn't a cop bound by laws and the Bill of Rights. He would give just about anything for the freedom to administer a little frontier justice right about now.

He read the dazed man his rights. Only when he was sure he wasn't going anywhere did Daniel pick up his own Beretta and Fox's weapon and turn to check on Rosa and Lauren.

Rosa was gazing at him with a wide-eyed kind of awe that left him highly uncomfortable. Lauren, on the other hand, looked ready to spit nails.

"Are you both okay?"

"We're fine," Lauren answered, her voice hard and tight. "You're bleeding."

He looked down and saw a red blotch spreading on his sleeve. He hadn't paid any attention to it in the heat of the moment, but now he realized his arm stung like hell.

"Did he shoot you?"

He flexed his arm. "Don't think so. I'm okay. I must have broken through my stitches from the other night when I was subduing him. I'll deal with it after I get Fox into custody."

Her mouth tightened. For a moment, he didn't quite understand the reason for her anger, and then he remembered everything, all he had told her the night before about her father's downfall and his role in it.

Of course. She hated him now. She was probably wishing Fox *had* shot him.

The satisfaction that churned through him at subduing and arresting Fox—at finding the man who had hurt Rosa and shot his deputy—dried up instantly and he was miserable once again.

* * *

She had never been so angry in her life.

The fury coursed through her like a thick, torpid creek and she couldn't seem to wade across it.

She managed to contain it while she treated Rosa for mild exposure and tried to follow the girl's story about what had happened earlier, about how she had heard a gunshot and climbed out the bathroom window and slogged through the snow as fast as she could looking for shelter.

She asked questions and made appropriate responses as best she could in Spanish, but the whole time she was afraid her fury would suck her under. The source of her anger was still in her clinic talking to Cale Davis and Gage McKinnon about what had happened.

She would have to give a statement soon, she knew, but right now her patient took precedence.

Rosa yawned suddenly in the middle of her story and Lauren forced her attention back to her patient, tucking the warmed blankets closer around her.

"Rest now," she said. "You can tell me the rest of the story later when Daniel is here."

Daniel was apparently the magic word. Rosa was crazy about him. The events of the last hour only seemed to have solidified the girl's hero worship.

Rosa nodded. Lauren smoothed a hand over her hair and she smiled, closing her eyes. She stayed with her until she fell asleep, then dimmed the lights and slipped out of the room, leaving the door ajar so she could hear if her patient awoke.

Out in the hallway, she finally let down her guard and leaned against the wall, utterly exhausted by the strain of the day and the sleepless night that preceded it. Her cheek and her head both ached where she had slammed against the wall and she closed her eyes, trying to relax the tight grip of tension in her shoulders with a couple of breathing exercises.

They didn't seem to want to be soothed, especially when some sixth sense warned her she wasn't alone.

She jerked her eyes open and found Daniel standing five feet away, watching her out of those intense dark eyes that missed nothing.

He looked so big and comforting and wonderful and she had to grip her hands together to keep from sagging against that hard chest and holding on tight.

Until she remembered how angry she was with him.

"Everything taken care of with Kendall?" she asked, her voice deliberately cool.

"Yeah. Cale and McKinnon will be picking him up at our jail and taking custody. Your Dr. Fox isn't going to be seeing the light of day anytime soon."

"He's not *my* Dr. Fox. I hope he never gets out of prison for what he's done."

He looked a little surprised at her vehemence, which only seemed to make her angrier. Did he honestly think she would have a shred of sympathy for Kendall?

"You need to let me look at your arm."

He glanced down with a distracted look, as if he had forgotten all about it. "I think it's stopped bleeding."

"I still want to check it out. Come in here."

She didn't give him a chance to argue, just headed for the nearest exam room. After a pause, he followed, looking about as thrilled to be there as a two-year-old on the way to a booster shot.

"Would you take off your shirt, please?" she ordered. The words had an oddly familiar ring and she couldn't figure out why until she remembered she had made the same request of him the night Dale Richins found Rosa in the bed of his pickup.

Everything had changed in those few short days. She had kissed him, touched him.

Discovered how very much she loved him.

She huffed out a breath. She wasn't quite

ready to surrender her anger yet by giving in to that soft twirl of emotion.

Still, she had to admit her insides shivered when he shrugged out of his uniform, baring that vast expanse of bronze skin and muscle.

She was a professional, she reminded herself. She shouldn't even notice. She stepped closer, and pulled the exam light over so she could look at his injury.

"The stitches still look good," she said after a moment while she rifled through a drawer of the exam table for the necessary supplies to clean off the crusted blood. "You must have just bumped it in a bad spot and started it bleeding again. I'm sure you were too busy being an idiot at the time to notice."

He raised an eyebrow. "Was I?"

"What else would you call it? You could have been killed, Daniel. He had a gun, in case it escaped your attention."

"I believe I was aware of that."

"What kind of idiot rushes toward a man holding a gun aimed at his chest?"

"It wasn't aimed at my chest when I tackled him, it was aimed at the door. I was well aware of the risks but I had everything under control. I had to take a chance, Lauren. I couldn't let him hurt you or Rosa."

"You were willing to sacrifice yourself for us!"

"It wouldn't have come to that. I wouldn't have let it."

Abruptly, all her anger seeped away, leaving only the echo of that raw, terrible fear she had endured watching him wrestle an armed and desperate man. She swallowed hard, hoping he couldn't see her hands tremble as she wiped gently around the edges of his injury.

"You could have been killed," she said softly. "I have never been so scared in my entire life."

To her horror, her voice broke on the last word. She took a breath, then another, trying to regain control, but it was too late. A sob escaped her and she dropped the gauze on the exam table and buried her face in her hands.

"Lauren," he murmured, then he wrapped those strong, wonderful arms around her and held her against his bare chest while she wept.

Those terrible moments replayed through her mind again and again, her fear and helplessness and the horrible dread when that single shot exploded through the room.

"Everything's all right now," he said. "We're all okay. You and Rosa are safe and that's the important thing."

Her hand curled into a fist and she struck out blindly, punching him in the chest, even though she was far too upset to put much force behind it.

"Don't you *ever* do that to me again, Daniel Galvez. I died inside when I thought he had shot you."

At her words, he froze, the hard, smooth muscles against her fist suddenly tight. After a charged pause, he covered her hand with his and drew it to his heart, squeezing tightly as if he didn't dare let go.

Her gaze lifted to his and the intense emotion there snatched away her breath.

"You did?" he asked, his voice low, shocked.

Her chin quivered as she nodded and wiped away a tear with her finger. Another one slipped out after it, but he dipped his head and absorbed it with a gentle whisper of a kiss.

"I'm sorry," he murmured, kissing away another and another.

"You'd better be," she replied, then she wrapped her arms tightly around his neck and drew his mouth to hers.

She kissed him fiercely, pouring every ounce of the emotion raging through her heart into her embrace. Love and anger and a deep, cleansing celebration of life.

Several long moments later, he lifted his head slightly, his expression dazed and his breathing ragged.

"You're going to have to take me back a few

steps here, Lauren. I must be a little slow this afternoon. I thought you hated me. After what I told you last night, I figured you would never want to talk to me again."

"I could never hate you."

"Ten minutes ago you were furious with me."

"I was angry at you for rushing a man with a gun, for risking your life. I still am."

During those long, terrible moments, all she wanted was the chance to tell Daniel how she felt about him. Now that she had the opportunity, the words seemed to catch in her throat.

She swallowed hard, then drew a deep breath for courage. "Mostly, I was angry because I couldn't bear thinking you might have died before I could ever tell you I love you."

Had she really just blurted that out? *She* was the idiot here. With her pulse pounding loudly in her ears, she finally lifted her gaze to his and the raw emotion in his eyes sent that pulse racing into what she was sure couldn't be a healthy rate.

He looked thunderstruck at first, completely stunned, then a fierce joy leaped into his eyes.

"Say that again," he ordered, his voice hoarse, stunned.

She managed a watery smile, tenderness soaking through her. She wasn't afraid of this. With everything inside her, she loved this man. Somehow she knew he would never hurt her. He had risked his life for her. Risking her heart was a piece of cake compared to that.

"I love you, Daniel. I think I have for a long time, I just never realized it until these last few days. I love your strength and your courage and your goodness. I love the way you touch me and the way you make me feel inside, like I'm riding a roller coaster without a seat belt, and the amazing way you seem to believe I can do anything I set my mind to do."

Daniel heard her words but he couldn't quite comprehend they were coming out of her mouth. He was afraid to believe it could be real, especially after the long, miserable night he had spent lying awake on her couch watching the flames dip and sway and wishing away the past.

He hated to ask, but couldn't seem to contain the question. "What about your father? About the investigation? You don't blame me for what happened?"

She sighed, looking weary. "How can I blame you for doing your job? My father made his own choices, every step of the way. You had nothing to do with them. I've had to accept that his choices had a ripple effect in many, many lives. I just never realized until today that some of those ripples have helped shape and guide my life into a direction I can't regret. I have a great life here. Good friends, patients I care about, a growing practice. No. I don't blame you."

Relief poured through him and he wrapped her in his arms again, resting his forehead on hers. He was at peace as he hadn't been in a long time and he wanted to hang on to the feeling forever.

"I have one more confession," he murmured.

She looked wary suddenly and he smiled, kissing her hard. "I have to tell you that when I was a kid, you were everything I ever dreamed of, everything I wanted. I think I was in love with you, even back then. Nothing has changed."

He stopped and shook his head slightly. "No, that's not true. *Everything* has changed. Before, I wanted this image I had of you, the perfect house and the pretty girl who went along with it. I didn't know that pretty girl would grow into this smart, incredible woman I love so much, someone who pours her heart and soul into healing others, who has this powerful sense of justice, a bottomless well of compassion in her heart. And a rather terrifying obsession with hot chocolate."

She laughed, though a faint wash of color danced across her cheekbones. He brushed his mouth across her soft, delicate skin. He couldn't believe this was real, that she was in his arms.

She loved him. It seemed a miracle, an incredible gift, and he was fairly certain his heart would burst with happiness. He smiled, not concerned in the least.

At least he would have a good doctor around when it happened.

Epilogue

"If you don't stop sniffling, she's going to hear you."

"I'm trying," Lauren whispered back to Daniel. She pulled out the handkerchief she had at least had the foresight to bring along, dabbed at her teary eyes, then shifted on the hard bleacher seats of the high school gymnasium trying to find a comfortable spot.

It wasn't an easy task for anyone—forget a woman who was six months pregnant.

Beside her, Daniel canted his hips slightly and

tugged her against him so she could use his solid bulk as a backrest.

"Better?" he murmured as the commencement speaker talked of lessons learned and the road less traveled.

"Much." She leaned into him gratefully, feeling the tight muscles in her lower back ease. After three years of marriage, she still couldn't understand how he instinctively seemed to know exactly what she needed before she even figured it out herself.

He did this kind of thing all the time, these quiet acts of consideration that always seemed to take her breath away. Her heart bubbling over with emotion, she reached for his hand, linking her fingers through his.

She would never have believed she could come to love him so much. She thought of the aching loneliness in her life before that January that had changed everything, before she acknowledged the feelings that had been growing inside her most of her life. She thought she had been content building her medical practice, living her life as best she could, trying to repair all that her father had done.

The contrast of these last three years to her earlier life only illustrated how starkly empty that world had been. Marriage to Daniel had been filled with everything she might have wished— laughter and joy and the peaceful assurance that this strong, wonderful man was crazy about her.

Not everything had been easy. Their early months together had been tempered by heart-ache as she had helped Rosa deliver her baby and then a day later handed the beautiful dark-eyed girl to the adoptive couple Rosa had selected.

More tears bubbled out now as she remem-bered Rosa's courage—and pain. Lauren was a physician, trained to help people heal, and she had hated knowing she couldn't make every-thing right for Rosa. Giving the child up for adoption had been the right choice. She knew it. But it hadn't been an easy one for any of them.

As an adopted child herself, she knew Rosa had been giving her daughter a better life than she could provide as a fifteen-year-old single mother with little education.

She and Daniel had talked long and hard about the possibility of adopting the girl themselves. In the end, Rosa made the decision for them, with a wisdom and strength that still amazed Lauren.

Here in Moose Springs, Rosa said, there would always be rumors swirling around her daughter. Everyone knew of the trial, of Rosa's violent rape and the attempts on her life. She wanted her child to grow up where she would never have to know the ugly circumstances that had created her, where she could be free to thrive and grow.

"My daughter is innocent of what happened to me and she should not have to live with that burden. No child should," Rosa had said firmly.

As it had been her choice, Daniel and Lauren stood by her and helped her find the right place-ment for the child. Rosa had finally selected friends of Daniel's sister Anna in Oregon, a wonderful, loving couple who had been childless for eight years.

Seeing their utter joy at their new daughter had eased some of the heartache, but not all. Still, the whole experience had given Lauren a new appreciation—both for the unknown woman who gave birth to her and for her own parents.

As the young speaker finished her speech with an enthusiastic plea to the graduates to grab all life had to offer, Lauren forced her attention away from the past back to the present.

"She's next," she whispered.

She didn't realize she was squeezing Daniel's hand so tightly until he laughed slightly and slid his hand away to cover her fingers with his. "Easy, sweetheart. She'll be great."

Jim Fordham, the principal of the high school, stood to introduce the next speaker and Lauren's heart kicked up a notch.

"Every year the senior class at Moose Springs High School votes on the most inspirational graduate of the year," the principal began. "It has been a tradition at this school since I attended, back in the Dark Ages. Never before could I say how wholeheartedly I support their unanimous selection."

He smiled as the crowd applauded. "This student exemplifies courage and strength under difficult conditions. She came into this country with barely an elementary school education but in two years, despite her circumstances, she has thrived. She does not have the best grades of anyone in her graduating class, but every teacher she has ever had at this school tells me no one tries harder to succeed. She is never without a smile, she is kind to everyone she meets, and she will be greatly missed by students and faculty alike when she leaves to attend nursing school on a full scholarship in the fall. Your choice as inspirational graduate of the year, Rosa Vallejo."

The graduating seniors jumped up and began clapping. Beside Daniel, Lauren thought her heart would burst with pride as Rosa walked to the microphone, her long dark hair gleaming against the glossy white of her graduation robes.

The frightened, battered girl she and Daniel had found in the back of Dale Richins's pickup was now a strong, beautiful, confident young woman. Rosa smiled at the crowd, though Lauren thought her gaze lingered on them for just a moment as she waited for the applause to fade and the crowd to sit again before she launched into her speech.

As Rosa began speaking in her accented but clear English, Lauren followed along in her head with the speech they had practiced for two weeks. It was a wonderful message and though Lauren had heard it dozens of times, she was still touched as Rosa talked of life's challenges, and how people can choose to wallow along in their adversities or they can reach out to lift others. She talked of the bright future and of possibilities in a speech punctuated several times by applause.

Close to the end, Lauren waited for the big inspirational finish. Instead Rosa's voice faltered.

She paused for several seconds, long enough that Lauren began to fear she had forgotten the words they practiced.

"I wish I had better English," Rosa said after a moment. "Maybe then I could find the words to thank the two people who have given me everything. They have given me help and courage, friendship, understanding, love. They have given me a home and they have stood with me through my darkest hours."

Rosa gave a watery smile and Lauren sniffled in response. Beside her, Daniel gripped her hand tightly. "Most of all, they have given me hope. My mother died in Honduras when I was thirteen. I did not know when I came to this country I would find two new parents but I have been so blessed. My heart is full of gratitude and love for them. To Daniel and Lauren Galvez, thank you. From the very, very bottom of my heart, I thank you. Because you reached out to help a stranger when you could have turned away, my future is a bright and wonderful place."

She stepped away from the podium and began to clap. Around them, others stood and clapped as well. This was her town, Lauren thought as she looked around at the smiling faces looking back at her. Her neighbors and friends and patients, and she loved them.

Daniel slid an arm around her and pulled her close and she risked a look at his strong, rugged features. Suspicious moisture leaked from his eyes and she handed the extra tissue she had brought along.

He would be a wonderful father to this child she carried. She had no doubt at all, because she had seen his quiet guidance with Rosa these last few years.

As the principal returned to the podium to begin reading off the names of graduates to hand out diplomas, Lauren touched her abdomen. Rosa was right. The future was a bright and wonderful place.

She couldn't wait.